Someone long ago once said the futur
But in reality, we found nothing but t

Everyone now says the past is ber
But in reality, all that was around us was a

Then where are our futures?
The answer is certainly nowhere but in these hands.

WORLDEND

WHAT DO YOU DO AT THE END OF THE WORLD?

ARE YOU BUSY? WILL YOU SAVE US?

2 Akira Kareno
Illustration by ue

Phyracorlybia

We know nothing but these skies and this city.

We cannot compare it to anything else, nor will we.

And yet—nay, that is the very reason why I can say this proudly: We love these skies and this city.

The fate of a blooming flower is only to shrivel and fall.

Yet, the little buds dance in the wind, dreaming of the day they will bloom.

One day, we'll be faerie soldiers like Miss Chtholly. ...One day is one day. A future a little further away than tomorrow.

I don't want to be scared. But what's even scarier is not being afraid of anything.

Lakhesh

Pannibal

There's nothing wrong with having one path. What's important is how you walk it. Right?

Tiat

No worries! Never fear— Collon is here!

Collon

"And you haven't changed a bit, have you?"

"Well, I've been stone this whole time. But it's incredibly touching to hear that from you, after how much you've changed."

"I'm not talking about your appearance. It's your nature—how you cannot leave young girls alone. I admire how this hasn't changed, even across eras, regardless of race."

"Don't talk in a way that'll give other people the wrong idea. You were like that a long time ago, too. You took good care of the little ones once."

"That's because Almaria was there. It's natural to put on a front before a woman you admire. Who on earth could bother with those irritating creatures if not for that?"

"Oh. I didn't know that's how you saw Al."

"—Wait. Don't get so bloodthirsty. This was a long time ago. I said wait!"

Willem

WORLDEND

WHAT DO YOU DO AT THE END OF THE WORLD?

ARE YOU BUSY? WILL YOU SAVE US?

#02

AKIRA KARENO

Illustrations by ue

YEN ON

NEW YORK

WORLDEND: WHAT DO YOU DO AT THE END OF THE WORLD? ARE YOU BUSY? WILL YOU SAVE US?

AKIRA KARENO

Translation by Jasmine Bernhardt
Cover art by ue

SHUMATSU NANI SHITEMASUKA? ISOGASHIIDESUKA? SUKUTTEMORATTEIIDESUKA? Vol. 2
©2015 Akira Kareno, ue
First published in Japan in 2015 by KADOKAWA CORPORATION, Tokyo.
English translation rights arranged with KADOKAWA CORPORATION, Tokyo through TUTTLE-MORI AGENCY, INC., Tokyo.

English translation © 2018 by Yen Press, LLC

Yen On
1290 Avenue of the Americas
New York, NY 10104

Visit us at yenpress.com ■ facebook.com/yenpress ■ twitter.com/yenpress ■ yenpress.tumblr.com ■ instagram.com/yenpress

First Yen On Edition: November 2018

Yen On is an imprint of Yen Press, LLC.
The Yen On name and logo are trademarks of Yen Press, LLC.

Library of Congress Cataloging-in-Publication Data
Names: Kareno, Akira, author. I ue, illustrator. I Bernhardt, Jasmine, translator.
Title: WorldEnd : what do you do at the end of the world? are you busy? will you save us? / Akira Kareno ; illustration by ue ; translation by Jasmine Bernhardt.
Other titles: WorldEnd. English
Description: First Yen On edition. I New York : Yen On, 2018– I Subtitle translated from Shumatsu Nani Shitemasuka? Isogashiidesuka? Sukuttemoratteiidesuka?
Identifiers: LCCN 2018016690 I ISBN 9781975326876 (v. 1 : pbk.) I ISBN 9781975326883 (v. 2 : pbk.)
Classification: LCC PZ7.1.K364 Wo 2018 I DDC [Fic]—dc23
LC record available at https://lccn.loc.gov/2018016690

ISBNs: 978-1-9753-2688-3 (paperback)
       978-1-9753-2690-6 (ebook)

10 8 6 4 2 1 3 5 7 9

LSC-C

Printed in the United States of America

WorldEnd

WHAT DO YOU
DO AT THE END
OF THE WORLD?

ARE YOU BUSY?
WILL YOU SAVE US?

WORLDEND

WHAT DO YOU
DO AT THE END
OF THE WORLD?

ARE YOU BUSY?
WILL YOU SAVE US?

#02

contents

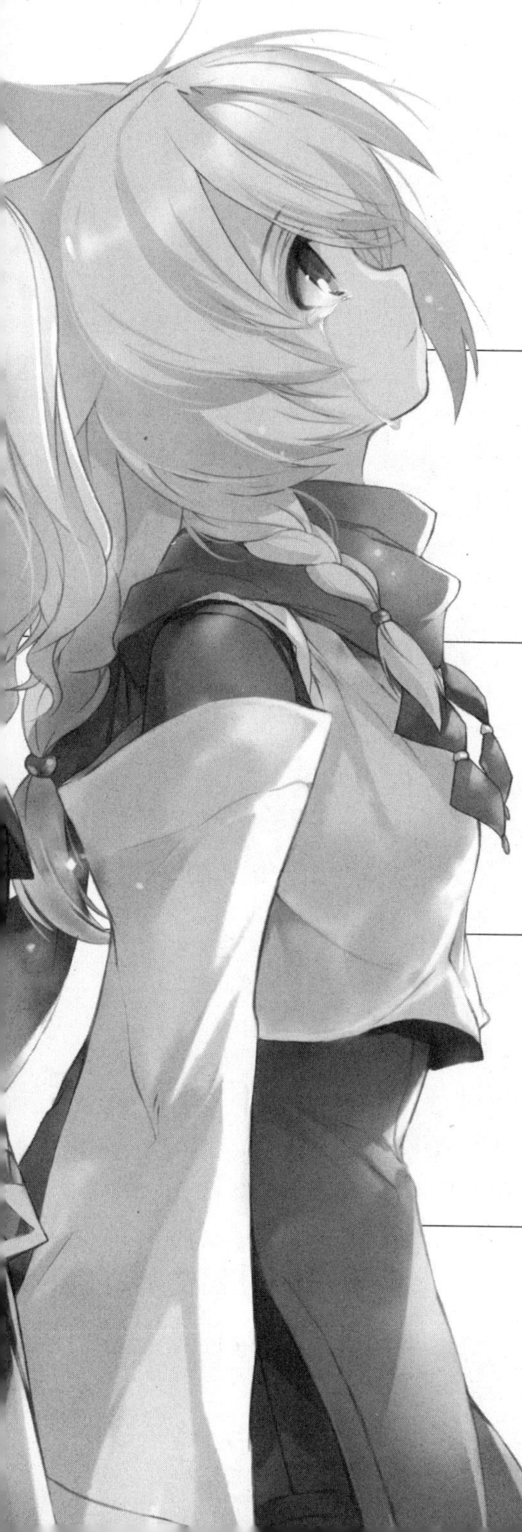

Now But a Distant Dream——A
-the fellowship-

Transport magic wasn't as convenient as society thought.

A magical rite tied two distant places together via enchantment, and "cargo" passed along the semi-physical corridor that opened through it. This allowed a long journey that would normally take months to be shortened and made it possible to send both people and things to faraway places— Well, certainly, hearing just that made it sound like dream technology. It even felt like this was the pinnacle of man's evolution.

But of course, the world is not so generous. Sometimes the location of the rite had to change depending on the position of the sun or the moon, or the ritualists had to activate their venenum almost to the point of being burned alive to make it work, or they had to take on the large burden when the subject of transfer was a living thing. A harsh reality always hid in the shadows of dream technology.

That was why there were only two types of people who could benefit from the transport magic on this continent: those from the communication bureau who needed to send crucial information quickly and a small portion of the military and adventurers who could change the tide of battle alone or in a small, elite team.

Outside of the Tihuana District on the edge of Empire territory, an abandoned cabin.

"Weren't we supposed to gather at noon?"

There were three people in the cabin.

Willem, one of the trio, looked around the room with a tired expression. No matter how many times he checked, there were only three of them, including himself. Four whole faces were missing from the number that should have been there.

"Are the others late? Oh, whatever."

"Wait, wait, wait! Why are you talking so calmly and shamelessly?! You only got here after the sun started setting!"

"And if you keep your mouth shut, the other four will never find that out."

"Where did you get that idea?! The truth won't change even if we decided to tell the same story, and we don't even have a reason to keep our mouths shut!"

"I don't really care, but can you stop screeching, Suowong? Cutting across the continent with transport magic has really given me a headache."

"And whose fault do you think that is?!"

After briefly raising his voice, the young thaumaturgist Suowong dropped his shoulders weakly.

Fluffy blond hair; light-blue eyes; a small, lean frame; and androgynous facial features: It might have seemed like his appearance would make him popular with the opposite sex, but regardless of time or place, he always wore the same pure-white cape, its hem dragging on the ground behind him, spoiling those good looks.

"Talking with you always ends up like this. I've never met anyone else who could break my stride like you—Black Agate Swordmaster."

"Haven't I told you to stop calling me that?"

"You're talking nonsense again. It's a stylish name; what are you unsatisfied with? Well, cool as it may be, it is, of course, vastly inferior to my true name—the Magus of the Polar Star. But I suppose nothing can be done about that, since that's a difference in ranking."

"Okay, just shut up already. Now you're giving me a different kind of headache."

"Hmph! What is that supposed to mean?!"

Suowong continued to grumble and complain, but Willem paid him no more mind and turned his gaze to the third person in the room.

"So you did come, Lillia."

"Hmm? *Whaya meen?*"

The girl, who was munching on biscuits as she read a book for some reason, looked up.

Her hair, red like burned bricks, wavered slightly.

"I told you it was okay to run away, didn't I?"

"Ahh, *that ahain?*" She bit into the pieces she had in her mouth. "Well, I had to come. If I don't do this, who will?"

"Me."

"Still saying that? But you can't."

He gulped.

Thrust before him was the naked truth, and he had no response.

"I'm sooo sorry I'm here on the battlefield without a care in the world. Gosh, I mean, I am an incredible genius overflowing with unprecedented talent, after all," Lillia said obnoxiously, then cackled.

Willem was dumbfounded, but what remained clear was the bitter taste in his mouth as he groaned in response.

"Look here, you…"

"Hey, that's not how you should be talking. Though it might be a fallen country, I'm still a genuine member of the royal family. Have some respect."

"Uh-huh. As for Her Highness, her character is as terrible as usual today."

"Oh my. Perhaps it's due to the rotten people around her? She must choose better companions with whom to spend all her time."

"Does she? Then I guess she won't be needing these." He produced a package of cookies from his pocket and waved it gently. "Almaria gave these to me for everyone to share, but I don't have any obligation to share with people who aren't my companions."

"Allie's cookies?!" Lillia lunged forward. "Willem, we're friends forever!"

"Ugh. Your personality, character, temperament, disposition, and even nature aren't worth commending. But I do sort of respect how quick you can switch up your attitude."

"And while you're respecting me, why don't you give me your daughter, Dad?"

"A Brave would never hand over his child to such a dangerous character."

"Hmm. Oh well."

Before she even finished speaking, Lillia had turned the bag inside out and emptied the contents into the biscuit tin.

"Those are for everyone. Leave some for Emi and the others."

"I know, I know." Lillia gave a noncommittal answer and began stuffing the cookies in her mouth. A moment later, Suowong yelled, "No fair!" and joined in.

"Come on, guys."

It was the usual banter among companions.

"...Hey."

"Hmm?"

"Why do you fight, Lillia?"

"That again? It doesn't really matter, does it? People can stand on the battlefield even without a reason, and they can fight well enough with the right talents. Isn't that good enough?"

"If you're serious, then sure, that's enough. I'm not convinced, but I'll accept it anyway. But just listening to the way you talk about it—"

"Makes it sound like I'm lying, you mean? What kind of lie?"

If he knew, then this wouldn't always be so difficult.

When it was clear there would be no response, Lillia smugly spat, "See? You should just keep quiet, stay behind me, and be my herald. Oh yeah, and do Seniorious's adjustments and that massage of yours. That's all you're worth, really. Just stick to what you're capable of."

She sniffed again arrogantly.

He didn't have a response.

There were lots of things he wanted to say. Like how her usual grinning mug looked like it was about to burst into tears for some reason—but he didn't know why that was, so he couldn't point that out.

No matter how much they fought together on the battlefield, no matter how much they joked around like they did just now, he never knew what Lillia was thinking.

"Hey."

"Hmm? Now what?"

"I really do hate you."

"Ohh."

Lillia suddenly broke into a wide, bright grin.

"I knew it!"

For some reason, she said that full of pride.

What was Lillia thinking about?

What was she hiding?

In the end, Willem never knew.

Those Who Wait, and Those Who Never Return

-dice in pot-

1. Time Since Then

He'd heard that the end of the hallway on the second floor was leaking recently.

When he went to go see for himself, he saw how it might need a little handiwork. Since they'd need to call in someone from town later for proper repairs, all he had to do now was just some emergency fixing up. He needed some wooden boards and—

"—Hey, you know where the hammer is?"

When he turned around to ask, no one was there.

Puzzled, he tilted his head.

There was a girl with hair the color of the cerulean-blue sky who had constantly been by his side recently. Her presence had become normal for him. Thinking she should have been nearby, he called out to her. But—

"Chtholly?"

He called her name, but there was no response.

Slowly, a feeling of unease welled up in his chest.

"Ithea? Ren?"

He called the names of Chtholly's two close friends, but still, no answer.

He put the repairs for the leak on hold and went to go look for them.

He walked around the building, from one side of the first-floor hallway to the other. His search took him through the reading room, the recreation room, training gear storage, the kitchen, and the dining hall. He went up to the second floor, meticulously checking each and every area.

He went outside. He walked through the forest. He searched the swamp. Heading even to the town, he peered inside every shop. The book-store. The watchmaker. The projection house. The accessory shop. The café. The butcher. They were nowhere. Nowhere to be found.

He drew aside some faeries he spotted and asked them. But all their answers were the same: *I haven't seen them. I don't know who that is. I don't know.*

Just as he cocked his head, puzzled, someone tapped him on his shoulder from behind.

He turned around, and there was a tall troll woman—Nygglatho, smiling sadly at him.

"You need to accept it already," she said, her voice gentle. "Those girls are dead."

Huh?

"You won't find those girls anywhere anymore."

Impossible. What was she talking about?

Regule Aire was, quite often, in danger of being on the verge of destruction.

With relative frequency, intruders from the wasteland below would be carried in by the wind. In order to fight back against them, the residents needed to rely on ancient superweapons, which could be activated and used in combat only by faeries who had the forms and hearts of young girls.

The entirety of the island cluster's destiny rested on the girls' tiny shoulders. It was a twisted, precarious world with an uncertain future.

"Have you forgotten? They were sent off to battle."

He remembered. He could never forget.

But he'd promised. Once she came home, he'd listen to anything she had to say.

When he told her to come back alive, she smiled and replied, *"Leave it to me."*

That was why she had to.

"You should get used to it soon. This is the natural course of things in this world."

It was a gentle voice, one for calming a disobedient child.

He followed Nygglatho's gaze and found her looking at four little faeries, who had gathered there at some point. The little ones, always running around without a care in the world, now stood in a row, oddly quiet.

Forced expressions still on their faces, the four stared straight at him.

They each carried familiar-looking swords in their skinny arms.

"We'll be back."

At that moment, a strong wind blew. He unconsciously shielded his eyes with an arm.

When he opened his eyes again, the four girls were gone.

A single white feather floated down before his eyes from some unknown place. But right as it was about to rest on the ground, another gust of wind came, and the feather was once again carried off into the sky.

"You should get used to it."

Nygglatho repeated herself, then simply closed her mouth.

Wait.

This isn't funny.

He should get used to it. He knew that, but get used to *what*?

Where was Chtholly? Ithea? Nephren? When would they be back?

The four girls—Collon, Lakhesh, Pannibal, and Tiat—where were they going with those swords? What were they doing?

He could not find the answers to his questions.

Of course, even if he did, there was no way he could accept them. Not even if he was being told he was only running from the truth, even if he was scolded for throwing a tantrum like a child.

"Face reality."

No. Stop. Don't say that to me.

If that was reality, then he no longer wanted to see it.

So Willem closed his eyes, plugged his ears, and began to recite the names of generations of Legal Braves to hide from his thoughts. The proper nouns he'd memorized as a child washed away all unnecessary thoughts in his head. Abel Melchera. Torven Schnoll. Vecker the Ruby. The Nameless in Black.

*   *   *

"—Twilla Nohten. Wily of the Rusted Blade—"

His eyes snapped open.

For several seconds, he stared blankly at the ceiling.

He looked to the window, spending another few seconds watching how the sunlight poured through from beyond the beige curtains.

"Foreigner Nils… Lillia Asplay…"

He pushed back the blanket and slowly sat up.

He cracked his neck.

He spent the rest of his time getting a grasp on the situation, and—

"I'm *so* glad that was just a dream!"

His voice wavered behind tears as he cradled his head.

✝

Not everything in his dream was a vision.

There was no mistaking that Regule Aire stood on thin ice. It was also true that the ones that held up the world were ancient curios and the girls who wielded them.

Chtholly, Ithea, Nephren. Three girls had left their home, bound for the site of a harsh battle. And he, Willem Kmetsch, who worked as manager for the faerie soldiers (at least nominally), had seen them off. There was nothing false about that story.

One more thing he noticed was how faithfully that dream matched reality.

Half a month had passed since the battle began.

The girls still had not come home.

2. On This Side of the Silver Screen

Two giant lizards stood facing each other, enveloped in a heavy mood.

One of the lizards was well built, wearing a military uniform with a stiff collar. Judging by the design, this one was male—a guy, rather. Judging by the elegant dress the other wore, it could be surmised that one was a lady.

They were silent, not exchanging a single word.

Behind them stood a row of old, historic stone buildings. The two stood on the arched bridge that crossed over the waterways cutting through the city.

The sun had long since set. The faint light from the gas lamps illuminated the pair against the darkness. There was no trace of another human soul—well, no, of course there wasn't—but without a sign of any other person, it was almost as though the entire world itself had disappeared, leaving only these two behind.

The lizard guy's tongue flitted out from his mouth.

The lizard lady's round eyes peeled back in surprise.

Some communication of intent had been conveyed just like that. The two gently drew closer together, feeling each other's warmth—was that a thing these cold-blooded creatures did?

What happened next made it seem as though they were being considerate of the pair's romantic rendezvous. The light from the gas lamps flickered, then finally went out.

The dark of night spread, gently enveloping the two lovers.

Then the story came to a quiet close—

Tink.

Once the day's performance was over, light from the illuminating crystals filled the projection room.

"Hmm." Pannibal nodded, as though she understood.

"Ooh." Collon seemed somewhat impressed.

"Wow..." Tiat's eyes glistened.

"..." Lakhesh's mouth was agape.

It was actually shocking how the little ones, who always ran around the faerie warehouse (the name of their lodgings) with such energy, had become quietly engrossed in the story, each expressing a different emotion.

Willem sat beside them, pressing against his temples as he fought a slight headache.

(...I have no idea what's going on...)

He knew, at least, that the projection he just watched was some kind of love story.

But he couldn't understand anything more than that.

In love stories, the audience should be able to empathize with one of the characters or at least enjoy it by admiring the beautiful cast of men and women. But this was a strange rendering where all the characters were lizardfolk, so the hurdles for both forms of appreciation were a little too high. The wall between races was truly a thick one.

☦

Just as the name implied, recording crystals were a special sort of quartz that could grab a clip of the surrounding scenery and record it. Depending on the classification and precision of the cut, purity, and size of the stones themselves, the accuracy and amount of what could be projected changed. By shining light with similar direction and wavelength, the recorded scene could be projected outward. By changing the angle even slightly, it was also possible to choose what images were projected, and when applying this logic, it was also possible to move the series of recorded imagery realistically during playback. The necessary equipment wasn't that expensive, so it was possible to install anything medium size and under in projection houses in town—it was all rather interesting.

Well, the technical stuff wasn't really important.

What mattered was that this technology existed on Regule Aire, and the recorded projection culture borne from it was spreading.

If the local projection house had all the right recording crystals, anyone could watch a performance they wanted to see without having to go all the way to a playhouse in the big city. The performances didn't have any sound, and the picture wasn't exactly clear, but at the very least, they existed. Performances played a major role in the spread of fiction within Regule Aire, but—

He exited the projection house, dragging the four little ones along.

"That was wonderful!" Tiat exclaimed, the air sparkling around her.

"Adults!" Collon exclaimed nonsensically.

"Mm-hmm!" Pannibal huffed, squaring her shoulders.

"One day, I also..." Lakhesh swooned, gazing into space.

Willem was the only one to sigh, his shoulders drooping.

It hadn't been very long since these girls had been "born" as faeries. Since they looked and acted like children no older than ten, when they wanted to visit the projection house, Willem was required to go along as their caretaker.

And that was how he had ended up accompanying the four girls.

"I'm exhausted..."

The outward appearance of the leprechaun girls was similar to the so-called featureless. They had no horns or fangs or scales or animal ears, and they bore a striking resemblance to the emnetwiht who once flourished on the surface. The only difference was that most of them had vividly colored hair and eyes.

So why did they feel this way after watching a lizard love story?

Perhaps it was their gender. Or their age. Or the difference in their generations. Or maybe everyone born on Regule Aire naturally enjoyed such things, and he was the only exception. *Ugh, there is no decency left in this world.*

"Um, is something the matter?"

He heard a considerate voice from somewhere below him.

Lakhesh was staring up at him, likely thinking something was wrong.

"Cheer up, Willie!"

The moment he thought something would come hurtling at his back, Collon's short arms and legs clambered swiftly up his right elbow and onto his shoulder. She was truly deft with that small body of hers.

"Yah! You gotta have guts! Guts!"

"Hmm, if you go for the carotid artery, you'll be golden."

"S-s-s-stop! Collon, come down quickly, and Pannibal, stop egging her on like that!"

Yes, Lakhesh was a good kid. And Collon and Pannibal were bad kids. Well, it was important for children to be energetic, so in that sense, they were all good kids. *By the way, that move really hurt, so how am I going to get her off?* His mind, still faintly hurting, was blank as he thought about that.

…Just then, he felt someone's eyes staring into his back, and he turned to the last girl.

"Tiat, what's wrong?"

"Huh?"

"Thinking about something?"

She seemed surprised for a moment, as though she wasn't expecting him to call to her.

"Well, um… I was just thinking that maybe, the reason you've been so down lately, is because of our seniors…"

"Your seniors? Oh, you mean Chtholly and the others?"

"Y-yeah."

That was interesting. It was a little odd to use the word *seniors* when referring to people who were essentially family.

But these faeries were still members of the Guard—more precisely, they were military assets. While they greatly differed individually, it wasn't odd for them to show they held some sort of respect for their elders.

"Well, sure, I guess so," he answered honestly, thinking there was no reason for him to hide it.

"Huh?" For some reason, Tiat raised her voice in surprise.

"It actually makes me anxious. I even had a weird dream this morning because they haven't come back."

"Even in your dreams?!"

"Whoa…"

Tiat (and, for some reason, Lakhesh) were dazzled.

They made the same faces as in the projection house, watching the lizard love story.

"…Wait, come on, guys. What are you thinking?"

"So you've been hiding your pain while waiting for your beloved to return?"

"Wow… Adult love…"

He had no idea what they were talking about.

"Ooh, a happy adult!"

"A sincere confession in the middle of traffic. You're brave, Manager."

He was even less sure of what the last two were talking about. But more importantly, his captive right arm was really starting to hurt.

"—It's normal to be worried about your family. Love and whatever isn't something to act so arrogant over. Aren't you worried about them at all?"

"Why?"

"What do you mean, why?"

"Even if we weren't worried, they would come home safely. And if it ends up they can't come back, then worrying won't solve anything," Tiat declared.

Oh—right. These girls were faeries. Lives meant to be consumed for war. And maybe because of that, they weren't particularly attached to their lives.

Did that indifferent way of thinking apply not only to their own lives but to the lives of other races?

(I'm guessing Chtholly broke that pattern, in a way.)

She said she didn't want to die.

Though she hadn't put it into words, her attitude told him she didn't want to expose the adorable little ones to danger.

In Willem's eyes, Chtholly's fear was a good thing. That way of life felt much more "emnetwiht-like" than even Willem himself, who couldn't see any value in continuing to live in this world.

He hadn't realized it, but the reason why he ended up supporting her might have been because of that.

"That's not what worrying is about." Since he couldn't move his right arm, he twisted his body to place his left hand on Tiat's head. "You'll understand soon enough."

"H-hey! Don't treat me like a child!"

"At the very least, Chtholly was worried. About you."

"...She was? Why?"

"Because she's an adult, I'd think. More than you are, at least."

Tiat puffed her cheeks up in a huff.

"Fine! Then we'll worry about them, too!" She faced the blue sky, shouting a declaration that didn't really hit the mark.

"Yeah!!" Collon cheered, like she didn't quite understand.

"Good luck," Pannibal chimed in, seeming like it didn't matter much to her.

"Adults... So Miss Chtholly really is an adult in Mr. Willem's eyes..." Lakhesh swooned as she murmured something to herself. He would pretend he didn't hear that.

"—Er, Collon. My ligaments and stuff feel like they're about to break. Get off."

"I haven't heard you cry *uncle* yet!"

"*Ohhh*, uncle, uncle."

"Woo!"

Slip. Collon jumped down lightly.

A cold wind blew through the town. His body was shivering ever so slightly, unbeknownst to him.

The sky was high above them, a few clouds here and there.

The seasons were slowly beginning to change.

✝

The facilities were deep in the forest on Island No. 68.

They were lodgings big enough for almost fifty people to live together, judging by appearances. It was a two-story wooden building that felt quite old. Right beside it was a tiny, well-groomed vegetable patch and flower bed. A little ways away was a recreational field, a bit on the small side.

On paper, this was a "warehouse" meant for storing the Guard's secret weapons. No one was supposed to live here outside of the bare minimum number of personnel needed to manage the assets.

Of course, "supposed to" meant that wasn't the case in reality.

More than thirty faeries lived their daily lives here.

The girls, who were nothing but objects on paper, were living their days so full of energy and cheer that it was impossible to think they were nothing but weapons.

On the roof of the "warehouse," a large bunch of laundry fluttered on the clothesline.

"—Oooh, the weather is looking bad."

A woman was glancing up at the sky, holding to her chest a sheet she'd just taken off the line.

"Hello, you delicious being. If you have nothing better to do, why don't you help me?"

"I'll help, so stop calling me that."

"What! It's the highest compliment among my people!"

"You all need to study the official language of the island cluster from scratch, right now."

As Willem responded with a joke, he lifted the woven basket that sat beside him and began to place the closest articles of laundry into it.

There was a slight dampness to the wind. The rain was approaching.

"Boo. I feel like you've been rude to trolls lately, Willem."

The woman puffed her cheeks like a small child. His cheek twitched slightly when he saw how much it suited her.

Nygglatho was one of the "bare minimum number of personnel needed to stay to manage the assets" mentioned earlier.

She looked to be about twenty. She was tall, her eye level roughly the same as that of Willem, a man. She was also a bit girlie, as she preferred to wear cute aprons and frilly dresses.

And of course, she wasn't a faerie. Just as she said herself, she was a troll. A massive, demonic race that lived as neighbors to people, exchanged smiles with them, and happily devoured them.

"Don't say it like it's a joke. I've been rude to you since the day I met you."

"How awful! What should I think of a man who says that seriously?"

Ash-colored clouds began to spread faintly in the sky. They should hurry.

They piled more sheets onto the mountain of laundry that spilled from the basket.

"You don't have to worry. You're the only person in this entire world right now who I can act like this around."

"Hmm. That was a strange pickup line. I think my heart just skipped a beat."

"I'll say it again—you and all your people need to go relearn the official language of this island cluster."

"Boo! But you talk to Chtholly and the others so nicely!"

Plop—a single raindrop left a gray smudge by his feet.

"Come on, move your hands not your mouth."

"I know, I know!"

They rushed around, taking down the laundry.

The rain poured as if from an overturned bucket.

Dark clouds that seemingly came from nowhere covered the entire sky. Though it was still early in the day, it was as dark as night outside.

"Just in time. We would've had to wash everything all over again if we took any longer."

They'd finished putting away the laundry and were now on their way to Nygglatho's room, upon her suggestion to take a tea break.

"And what is it you need?" Nygglatho suddenly asked as she lit the fireplace.

"Huh?"

"Didn't you come to me on the roof because you needed something?"

"Oh..." Now that she mentioned it, she was right. "Well...I was just thinking, shouldn't we be hearing whether or not they're all right at some point soon?"

"Oh, you mean Chtholly and the others?"

That was exactly right. He nodded silently.

"I believe I heard this fight would take exceptionally long."

"I heard that, too, but it's been two weeks! Aren't we going to hear anything, like if they're okay or how much longer it'll take?"

"No."

"Why the immediate response?!"

"Why? Well, that's just the way it is... Do you wish to hear the details?"

He sat down silently in the chair she motioned to with her gaze.

She began to place the tea set, which seemed to magically appear from thin air, on the small table.

"You know about the girls' enemy, Timere, yes?"

"Only a bit from documents. Its properties are unknown, a tenacious thing, and its size and strength are in direct proportion."

"Yes. It is so tenacious because it grows and divides so quickly. No matter how much we kill, it uses its own corpse as a shield and creates a new self from the insides that aren't dead yet. Not only that, but it actually gets a little stronger every time. Still, if they're fighting against its small pieces as they always do, then it will reach its division limit if they persevere and kill every piece at least ten times. But the size of it now could easily exceed two hundred layers, so that will take some time."

Of course, the girls wouldn't be fighting twenty-four hours straight every day. They would come fully prepared, knowing it would be a long battle. A large number of the stalwart lizardfolk artillery forces would be accompanying the faeries in order to buy them time to rest.

So while it was tempting to just tell the muscly lizards to fight on their own, the enemy could not be substantially damaged if not for the faeries equipped with the Carillon, and since that was the very reason the faeries existed in the first place, there was not much that could change that.

"Since we've decided not to have Chtholly open the gates to the faerie homeland, it's only a question of whether they can keep fighting until they've dismantled the final shell. However, there is no way to tell how many layers of shells there are or how many they've destroyed so far. That is why there is no telling how much longer the fight will last."

Nygglatho continued, stating lightly that it would end someday, and that since they had managed to dominate it with basic firepower, then the odds weren't too bad.

"Then they should at least notify us if they're still okay."

"They've covered the area with layered control encampments, so without airships flying, communication crystals won't work, either. And on top of that, the air currents around the area are irregular, so the option of having winged races do some work is also out. The most we can do is confirm from a very far distance that the fight is still going on." Nygglatho fiddled with her red hair, twirling it around the tip of her finger. "Well, that's apparently why we receive no contact when the girls are fighting. I asked almost the exact same things you did when I first came here. And the answer I got was almost just the same as I've told you. Is there anything else you want to ask?"

"...No." He dropped his shoulders. "You look awfully calm about this right now. You used to it?"

Nygglatho sighed deeply. "Not entirely. My heart is pounding. I haven't had any appetite."

He would have been overjoyed to hear that if he took it out of context.

"But no matter why, the elders shouldn't be the first to panic while the littlest ones are just going about their business, yes?"

"Well, sure."

The kettle on the fire began to steam.

He watched Nygglatho out of the corner of his eye as she ran about preparing the tea and muttered sullenly, "I'd no idea doing nothing but waiting would be this hard."

Nygglatho painted a grin over her worried expression. "Glick told me you were saying such slick things at first. That you trusted the children, so you would accept whatever outcome."

"Not just at first. I haven't changed my mind since then. But...I didn't think it'd take this long back then. I'm not uneasy or depressed or any-thing. I'm just…starting to worry."

"Just starting to worry?"

"Just starting to worry. Something wrong with that?"

"Nothing wrong or right, it just feels like your cool and enigmatic character image is starting to fall apart *again*." A pensive look crossed her face. "Oh—I see; I understand. You're actually the type who can't put up a tough front unless it's your own territory, correct?"

"Gh—"

"That is why you don't know what to do in situations you're not used to and can only run about in confusion. You're quite the stereotype of a boy who has no confidence in himself."

"Urgh—"

That was a terrible way to put it, but sadly, he couldn't argue.

Nygglatho folded her arms on the desk and rested her chin on top.

"—So flustered and overwhelmed. I'm having so much fun just watch-ing you right now," she said, casually gouging out his heart.

"You're a demon."

"I am a demon. You were mean to me earlier, so this is my payback." The troll teasingly stuck out her tongue. "Let me just say this while you're treating me like a demon, but if you stay idle at times like these, your mind will never stop racing in circles. One way to deal with it is to change your environment or even overwhelm yourself with things to do."

"Hmm. I know your motives. You want me to ask for work, don't you?"

"That is correct."

The demon grinned, satisfied.

Willem thought. Though there was a joking manner to their conversa-tion, there was some truth in what the demon woman said.

Continuing to worry about Chtholly and the others itself wasn't a bad thing. But he had originally planned to spend his days like he always had. And so, he was going to wait for them, just as his family had waited for him to come home, back at the now long-gone orphanage.

Then there was some value in going along with this plan.

So that he may wait, immovable, for them to come home.

"Fine. What are you going to make me do?"

When he responded as such, Nygglatho clapped her hands together.

"It's a little far, but there's somewhere I want you to visit," she said.

3. Ancient Cities and Ancient People

Tiat had a dream.

She was in a place she had never been, looking at scenery she had never seen, talking to someone she had never met. That kind of dream.

No one would think this odd from that alone. Dreams were often like this. If one could dream about actual events, then one could also dream of strange, illogical fantasies.

But for the faeries, it was a different story.

It was almost like they *knew* it was a special dream the moment they opened their eyes. Without rhyme or reason, they strongly believed it was fundamentally different from normal dreams, where being warm, being scared, having fun, being sad left no marks on the real world.

And they knew it was an omen.

✝

She said it was just a little *far.*

Now that he thought about it, he should have checked with her then. How far did *a little* mean, exactly?

He left the island, transferred airships several times, and spent almost a full day in the air.

Just as he was on the brink of exhaustion from traveling all day, Willem finally reached his destination.

Island No. 11, the city of Collina di Luce.

It smelled like stone.

That was the first thing he noticed when he exited the airship gangway.

More specifically, it smelled like stone and brick that held a long history, like cobbled streets that had been stepped on for years, like the people who lived there, like the wind that blew through the town.

There was a market square right by the aire-port. It was apparently the market day, and he could see weathered canvas tents lined neatly in a row. Beyond it was a townscape of vivid reddish-browns and grayish-whites.

Various races of people passed through the town in relatively equal numbers. If he had to pick, it did seem like there were more lycanthropes than others, but even that was nothing more than a hunch. He also caught glimpses of other featureless like Willem himself. It didn't seem like there was any need to conceal himself with hoods or hats.

"...Wow." He unwittingly made a sound in admiration. "That's a surprise. It's way more like an ancient city than I imagined."

He'd heard stories about it. With a history of more than four hundred years, it was the oldest city in Regule Aire. It was an unusual place that, in all its time, had never been exposed to the fires of war or been destroyed by invaders from the surface.

That being said, Regule Aire was in the sky to begin with.

Elves would never come attacking from the woods nearby, nor would a sudden surge of orcs come from beyond the horizon. There were no worrying dragons, who spent their idle time burning down houses, and the dreadful Visitors who declared the purge of the entire emnetwiht race were no longer around. By this point in time, nearly everyone had experienced the fires of war.

Also, being in the sky meant that materials were limited. Quarrying stones from the islands, in particular, would essentially mean they were cutting away at the very land they lived on. Naturally, building stone became a comparatively expensive construction material. And a stone-built town used up more than what met the eye.

That was why when he heard this was the oldest among the most prominent cities in Regule Aire, he glossed over it, thinking it was nothing compared to the cities that once existed on the surface. It looked like he was going to have to think over how he'd scorned it.

A golem that looked like a barrel had sprouted arms and legs ran about restlessly, carrying a wooden crate. Willem stopped to make way for it so they wouldn't crash, and after a brief "Thank you," it hurried off. Towns thriving in tourism and trade really were a bit different if they were even adding amiability to their golems' artificial intelligence.

As he thought about this and that, he began to walk.

"Wha—?"

When he noticed his traveling companion wasn't by his side, he whirled around.

"—*Wooooow*—"

There stood Tiat, at the top of the airship gangway, the air around her glittering.

Her mouth hung wide open, a mixed expression of delight, surprise, and awe on her face. As if it weren't enough, she had entirely spaced out.

"Hey, c'mon. Let's go," he called to her, but she didn't respond. Her consciousness had flown off elsewhere.

"Hey." He went back up to her and flicked her forehead with his finger.

"Ow!!"

"Let's get going. I'm tired from sitting and traveling all day. Don't make me work."

"B-but this is Island No. 11!! The city of Collina di Luce!! The real thing!!"

"Uh, yeah."

"A place of history! The jewel box of the azure sky! The melting pot of romance and legend!"

She was talking passionately about something. A melting what?

"There are so many stories that use this city as a setting!"

"You've been acting like this everywhere we've gone since we left No. 68. Every single time we've had to transfer, you look around so dazzled like this."

"That's because I've never left the island before... No! This island and this city are special! An exception!"

She insisted frantically as she broke into a jog and caught up with Willem.

He felt the eyes of the surrounding people gathering on them. The alienating looks given to featureless— No, gentle, appreciative gazes for a heartwarming family outing. They must have been looking at them like a brother and sister from an island on the outskirts who were visiting the city for the first time.

Well, that interpretation wasn't entirely wrong.

Those girls lived in such a small world, and their universes were limited to the things they saw in books and projections. She probably couldn't help getting so excited just by leaving the island. Not only that, but this place apparently set the stage for some of her favorite stories. He sort of understood why she was in such high spirits.

"Okay, let's go. We didn't come here to sightsee, y'know."

He sort of understood, but they would get nowhere even if he did respect it.

"Awww, let me indulge a little bit—come on!!"

He tugged on her small hand and began to walk. Her chuckle tickled his back. He thought he was used to being so conspicuous, but for some reason, he just couldn't stand this atmosphere.

"Ooh, h-hey, can we see that up close?!"

"...What?"

Tiat was gazing at a large plaza, a fountain, and—

"The statue of the great sage of Falcita Memorial Plaza!"

Standing majestically in the center was the statue of an old man.

"Yeah, but..."

He narrowed his eyes and observed the statue. The old man wore an intrepid expression and a hood over his head.

While it might be something artistic, Willem had always been clueless about that sort of stuff. He never really understood emnetwiht art, so there was no way he could ever assess art made by other races. He could have at least made some sort of comment from a man's point of view if it was a female statue, but since it was of an old man, he couldn't.

"What is that?"

"It's a bronze statue of the person who founded this town a long time ago and a classic rendezvous spot for lovers! It sets the stage for so many stories!"

"Stage?"

"Like, in the last scene of *The Stars and Wind of Collina di Luce*, Rust-nose was eating fried potatoes, remember?"

It sounded like Tiat wasn't interested in the statue for its artistic value.

"I heard a legend that if two lovers give their vows for eternal love before the statue, then they'll be happy for five years…"

"That doesn't sound like a very great legend."

Though they're supposed to be vowing for eternity, what would happen on their sixth year together? *No, that doesn't matter right now.*

"No sightseeing. Don't forget—you came here for a mission."

"Urgh…"

That sounded like it was enough to remind her of her position. She lowered her left arm, which she had been waving about in excitement, and dropped her shoulders, too.

"You're going to be a great faerie soldier one day, like Chtholly."

"Oh, yeah. That's…right. I didn't forget."

She turned her gaze downward, wriggled her right hand free from Willem's grasp, and walked off, dragging her feet.

"Let's go."

Willem stopped in his tracks. Tiat took ten steps before turning around to look at him.

"What is it?"

"Well…our airship back is scheduled for tomorrow evening."

"And? So?"

"Once our mission is finished, I'm sure there'll be time to take a bit of a walk around."

"..."

It didn't seem like she understood right away what he meant.

Slowly but surely, Tiat's mopey expression transformed into a big, bright smile.

She trotted the ten steps back to Willem and snatched his hand.

"C'mon, no dillydallying!"

Yes, my lady, I know.

He bit back his smile and let her lead the way.

Shiver.

Suddenly, a small, odd sensation caressed the back of his neck.

It was a familiar feeling, reminding him of when he worked as a Quasi Brave on the surface.

(...Spite...?)

It wasn't from just a single source. Several people harbored animosity toward several others. A faint tension, characteristic of the moments just before a dispute, filled the air.

That being said, the scale wasn't that big, and they weren't the targets of the animosity.

"What's wrong?"

"Hmm? Oh, nothing."

Even in this place, a peaceful tourist spot at first glance—or perhaps *because* it was a peaceful tourist spot at first glance—lurked the seeds of trouble.

(Well... Whatever...)

He wasn't in the business of going out of his way to deal with troubles that weren't headed in their direction.

He decided to let it go and let himself be led through the city.

✝

No one could stand up to the Beasts that were destroying the world without a Carillon.

However, only emnetwiht chosen by the Carillon could use them.

And before even the question of whether or not one was chosen, the emnetwiht as a race were wiped out centuries ago.

So the Beasts could not be stopped. The world was ending.

People were not apt to take such simple logic lying down.

The emnetwiht no longer existed? Then they should simply use a replacement.

There was a race that could do that. There was a small natural phenomenon that lived near emnetwiht since time immemorial, used emnetwiht tools, and helped with emnetwiht work. Things born from the souls of children who died young, as a result of not understanding their own deaths and wandering astray through this world.

Those in the old world were said to take the form of little people no taller than knee-height, but those born in this world took a more human form—specifically, that of young girls. The reasons for such a change were unknown, but it was the perfect form to make them use weapons. And even with this different form, it was likely that their true nature always remained the same:

To stay by the emnetwiht's side. To help them.

To follow in their steps and copy their work.

They were born for such purposes and would disappear for such purposes.

"...However, it isn't that every single faerie is able to use dug weapons. While it seems all of them have the proper makeup itself, they won't bloom if they're too young."

"Huh."

His neck hurt.

The man sitting before him was a giant.

His broad figure, more than double Willem's size, was bursting with muscle.

He was also bald, had fangs, and wore a lab coat, and the single eye behind his (probably custom-made) black-rimmed glasses glittered intelligently—and his title was *Doctor*.

"This is a general clinic owned by Orlandry. Regule Aire's best equipment and medicine are located here. Faeries who dream of omens come here, and we carry out adjustments to their bodies so that they may fight as mature faerie soldiers. Dug weapons are rare, and our foes are mighty. Nothing good comes from forcing a faerie to hold a sword and pushing them to their limit when their body isn't ready."

His voice was soft and gentle, and he spoke logically. His physique, on the other hand, was nothing but monstrous. Willem just couldn't wipe away his unease.

"...So where's Tiat now?"

The ceiling in the room was exceedingly high, probably built to accommodate the doctor's body. Willem thought absentmindedly that this was how it must feel for cats and dogs living in a human-size world.

"She is undergoing her physical examination right now. The female doctors are taking care of it in the other room."

"And so why is it that you, her attending physician, are just sitting around here?"

"I leave all work that can be done by others to others. Anything else, I'll do personally. Right now, I want to talk to you, Willem Kmetsch."

Willem cocked his eyebrow. He hadn't even introduced himself yet.

"No, no, no. No need to be so cautious." The giant doctor waved both hands. "I didn't find out about you by any suspicious means; I simply heard the story from Ny's letter."

Ny? ... Oh, Nygglatho.

"Those are some really suspicious means, don't you think?"

"Now that you mention it, it certainly seems that way."

So he agreed. Willem felt a little bad for Nygglatho saying it out loud.

"Anyway, you—"

From far away, he could hear a faint explosion that cut off the giant's words.

It repeated three times at roughly even intervals.

"A gun?"

"Sounds like it. Probably the Annihilation Knights."

"...Sorry. I'm not really used to the official language, so I didn't hear you very well. The what?"

"Annihilation Knights."

"What kind of knights are those? That sounds like the name of someone who got a little too reckless in their youth and came to regret it five years later."

"It's a group of young people who act out here and there because they aren't satisfied with the current mayor's policies. They've merely declared themselves as *knights*, but their backers are members of former nobility, so they're surprisingly legitimate."

"Huh."

I see. That's where the animosity I felt earlier was coming from.

"Either way, there's nothing calm about guns. Is it like the friction between progressives and reactionaries?"

"Something like that. This was a semifer city a long time ago, but they had strong territorial tendencies. They insist that the history of this town is also their history and don't think it a very good thing to interact with other races."

"Wow."

History. History, huh?

He recalled the people who lived in the capital in the world long ago. Though it only had a history just short of two hundred years, the majority of the people who lived there were proud of, or rather attached to, their city.

"—Pride is essentially the same as arrogance. You prove your worth by associating yourself with something of value. That self-satisfaction can make you stronger.

"You hear it a lot: Medicine can be poison depending on how you use it; the same is true of the reverse.

"Pride is no different. It can be beautiful or ugly depending on how you use

it. You oughtta drill that into that head of yours, since luckily or not, you happened to be born to a noble house."

He brushed away his master's words that started recounting in his head. Everything he said sounded like that, and it clung to the corners of his mind, refusing to go away. Those words were meant for his other student in the first place, and he had just stood by her, listening.

"Tradition may as well mean nothing in a city where you hear gunfire in the middle of the day."

"It's not uncommon that intentions don't match up in larger organizations. And surprisingly, the higher-ups might not think it a problem if outsiders will stop getting close."

"I see."

It sounded plausible, so he nodded honestly after a moment of thought.

"Four hundred years of history is probably nothing to you, who's lived for more than five hundred."

The giant doctor, seemingly unsure of how to handle a moment's silence, made a strange remark.

"...I spent five hundred years doing absolutely nothing; you can't call that history. I'm not arrogant enough to compare the two."

"Such modesty."

"Bragging about how long you overslept is just shameful. And..." He faltered.

"And— Yes?"

The giant pressed him on with a smile.

A cyclops's smile was frightening. It was enough to make any child cry and, at worst, would probably scar them for life.

Willem wasn't a child, nor was he afraid, and yet—

"...It's nothing."

He waved his hand, dodging the issue.

"Hmm?"

The giant's single eye narrowed, as though trying to peer into Willem's mind.

"Well, sure. Regule Air must be like a dream world to you. It would not be strange if you felt disjointed from reality, as if everything seemed manufactured. It may not mean much for you to hear this world is four hundred years old."

"I didn't say that!"

"I see. My apologies, then."

He shook his giant body lightly with a shrug.

There was a knock at the door, and a lizardfolk wearing a lab coat entered the room.

Out of all the races, the lizardfolk had the greatest variance in individual physique, but this one was a little on the small side. The short lizardfolk gave Willem a slight bow, handed the giant a number of documents, then left the room.

"...The results of Tiat's examination are here."

"Can I ask?"

"Of course you may. Let's see..."

He adjusted his glasses.

He read it aloud along with his notes. Basically, her physical development was appropriate for her age, and her health was excellent. The only problems were the heavy burden on her digestive system from drinking too much milk and that several teeth seemed to be at risk of developing cavities.

"I'll tell her to be more careful," Willem responded, rubbing his temple with his finger.

A few things came to mind. Tiat would exclaim at every opportunity, "I'm gonna grow!" and down an entire glass of milk in one gulp—and each time, she would end up coughing and spluttering. She also had a bigger sweet tooth than the average person. It was incredibly embarrassing to be confronted with this again.

"Even the encroachment from her previous life, which was our biggest concern, has stalled at a low level. Yes, I believe she will be a wonderful faerie soldier."

"...Encroachment?"

"Yes, encroachment. Without exception, all the girls are reincarnated beings, or rather, souls of the deceased themselves. They were someone else before being born into their current form. It can have grave influences on their personality and physical body when those memories remain or if they recall them."

Willem found himself perplexed at how smoothly the man gave the explanation before there was even a chance to think about accepting the explanation itself.

"That's more in the territory of ritual magic than medicine, isn't it? Are medical staff nowadays dabbling in necromancy, too?"

"All knowledge that can help in a patient's recovery is medicine. Right?" the doctor said, the corners of his mouth lifting. That was apparently a joke.

"Well, you won't need to worry about rituals, especially when it comes to Tiat. She'll stay herself. She's in good condition."

"Fine, then."

—*Something's not right.*

He felt slightly uneasy, like a small bone was caught in his throat. But he didn't know why.

✝

It sounded like he would have to leave Tiat at the clinic for a full day so they could adjust her physical properties appropriately for the purpose of one day becoming a faerie soldier.

Willem must have looked blatantly uneasy when they told him they would be medicating her and using hypnosis.

"No need to worry—it won't hurt her. All faerie soldiers compatible with dug weapons have walked this path before."

When he heard that, he knew he couldn't start raising a fuss over nothing.

"I'm gonna grow up splendidly, so you better keep your hopes up!"

Tiat gave Willem a thumbs-up with such energy, and he lightly patted her head.

"I don't think you're gonna grow any taller after adjustment," he whispered to her.

"Th-that's not what I was hoping for! I'm serious!"

Her face was bright red as she insisted, and with a smile, he saw her off. A smile he managed, somehow.

"I'm gonna grow up splendidly, so you better keep your hopes up!"

What are we hoping will happen once she grows up healthy and strong?
It's obvious. She'll go to the battlefield.
Fighting as a weapon, being consumed, and eventually losing all her strength.
Being born, raised, and completing her "life" as a weapon.
This world is slowly heading toward its doom.
My story ended a long time ago.
And now, I have a hand in their end.

"This isn't a good thing to think about."

He shook his head lightly and searched for the night's lodgings.

4. One Outcome

After a dreamless sleep, Willem greeted the morning alone.

Physically, he was in great shape. But emotionally, everything felt terrible.

"...I just can't shake this."

Laying back on the soft bed, he let out a low sigh.

It was probably this bed's fault for making him think nothing but bad thoughts.

The mattress must have been pretty expensive, as his back sunk deeply into it. It felt wrong.

The canopy was high and had impressive engravings of giant dragons on it that also made him uneasy.

This was the commander's dayroom in the city of Collina di Luce's Winged Guard Command Headquarters.

It was a dayroom only in name, as the size and facilities made it a splendid bedroom.

Willem had never received any education as an officer, nor did he ever receive any distinctions on the battlefield. But through a special (not respectable) circumstance, he came to hold the distinguished title of second enchantments officer. Upon showing his ID and an introduction letter from Nygglatho, he was offered this room to stay in while on duty.

Second officer's a big deal, huh...?

It was only now that such a silly thing felt real.

People in high positions typically needed good reason to be appointed to their offices. Without some combination of skills, wealth, or nepotism, it was unlikely they would succeed. This room was meant for those who had overcome all that.

He had no idea how Glick had managed to put him in the position of second officer in the first place. Considering how there'd been no problems thus far, it didn't sound like it was just simple document forgery or doctoring.

Either way, there was no doubt that his position and privileges didn't match up with his actual worth. Because of that, he felt sorry, because it was almost like he was tricking the honest soldiers here, making him feel ill at ease.

"I'll go take a walk..."

He was to pick up Tiat in the evening. There was plenty of time.

The reason he'd come to such a faraway island in the first place was to make sure he wouldn't overthink with all the time he had on his hands. So there was no point in his lazing about in the room. He should at least take a look around this city, supposedly renowned as the melting pot of romance and legend.

"I hope I can drag Tiat around before we go back..."

She had been so excited, after all. He would feel so bad for her if they only ended up lost and wasting all their time after they finally had the chance to sightsee—or, rather, it would probably be a bit of a pain to drag her all the way back to Island No. 68 if she was dejected like that.

So it probably wasn't a bad idea to do some sightseeing beforehand.

He chuckled softly to himself and felt a little lighter.

It was only when he came to the hall leading to the front entrance that he realized.

The townscape spreading outside was starting to grow black in dampness.

It was raining.

"Why does it have to start raining *now*?"

Part of the ceiling was leaking in a corner of the hallway, and there was a big bucket placed beneath it.

The buildings looked magnificent from the outside but were indeed weathered with the seasons and starting to show their age in some places. Boggards in military dress looked at one another and began asking where the wooden boards and the hammers were.

"Well… There's an elegance to an old city in the rain, so this probably isn't too bad."

He could probably borrow an umbrella from the headquarters here. If not, then he could just buy one at a nearby gift shop. Then—

"Eek!"

His response came a little late as he was looking up to the sky, thinking.

He almost ran headfirst into a woman who jumped in through the front entrance.

In the few moments before his consciousness could react, the conditioned reflexes instilled in him began to propel his body automatically. It recognized the woman's movements as an enemy attack, moved his body out of her way with the slightest shift, then slipped into her blind spot. As she was about to fall over, he set his aim on the nape of her neck and began to lower his hand in a chop—

Just as he was about to do so, Willem's consciousness finally held back his reckless reflexes.

"Oops."

He pulled his chopping hand back, wrapped it around the woman's waist, and held her up. "Eep!" She gave a little cry.

"Um, ah…"

"That was close. Don't I always tell you to watch where you're going when you—? Uh, never mind."

Willem's habitual scolding tone had accidentally come right out of his mouth. When he realized that she wasn't one of the little faeries, he cut himself off with a wry smile.

He stood her up on the spot and let her go.

It was a lycanthrope girl.

Her whole body was covered with a light coat of soft white fur. Her facial structure resembled that of the proud wolf. It was only her pointed ears that were wrapped in the color of lightly burned straw. Judging by the well-made silk dress she wore, she was probably from a good family.

Why had this young lady run, in the middle of the rain, into a military establishment? She didn't seem like a soldier, but if the guards had let her through the gate, then she must at least be authorized in some way.

"Thank…you…?"

With an expression that suggested she still didn't quite understand what had happened, the girl bowed her head politely. Just that one elegant gesture alone indicated she really wasn't suited to this place.

"It's dangerous to run around without looking where you're going, especially in a military facility. You never know where there might be dangerous materials."

"Oh, yes, my apologies."

He gave her a rough nod in response.

"Well, I'm off."

Willem decided to leave immediately.

He hated trouble, especially when women and kids were involved. He couldn't just run away. There would be no forgiving himself if he admitted defeat once a woman or child asked him for help. It was probably—no, it was *definitely* because of his master's instruction. He was living with his master's teachings in his blood and flesh.

That was why the moment he caught a whiff of trouble, the best option was to run away before anyone could ask for help.

He'd always been told it was a crooked way of thinking or that his kindness was half-assed. He knew that. But anyone who didn't have good control over their own mind looked crooked and half-baked by those around them. *So I'm not wrong, and it's not my fault. I'm out.*

"U-um, excuse me!"

He was still there.

His back still toward the girl, he turned only his head around, like a rusted screw.

"What is it? I'm not gonna apologize for touching you."

"No, that was my responsibility, so I shall put away my blade."

"I see, well, I'm glad you're so understanding... Wait, a blade?"

The girl ignored Willem's question.

"That is not it. I have something to ask of First Officer Limeskin, so would it be possible to get an audience with him?"

"Lime... Huh?"

That name sounded familiar.

The large lizardfolk man with milky-white scales. The very man who commanded the faeries and took them to the battlefield. Second Enchantments Officer Willem Kmetsch's direct superior on paper.

But now—

"That big lizard is at war far beneath the sky right now."

He'd taken Chtholly and the others to fight off Timere, which had drifted ashore to Island No. 15. And there was no end in sight for that battle.

Well, no, that wasn't quite it.

In principle, islands with nearby numbers were also close in distance. This was Island No. 11, so it wasn't unreasonably far from Island No. 15.

He could probably get there sitting two hours by airship. So it was a bit of an exaggeration when he said "far beneath the sky"—but he wasn't going to bother correcting himself.

"When do you think he will return?"

"No idea. If anything, that's what I wanna know." That was the truth. "Assuming that they've set up encampments in layers or whatever, all communication is blocked. We'll only hear from them when everything's been settled. It's doing a number on my heart."

"I…see…"

Her shoulders and ears drooped. She was easy to read.

"Well, if you need something, go ahead and grab one of those soldiers there—"

He motioned with his chin to some boggards who just happened to pass by.

He heard a clamor.

The building began to rumble violently.

Soldiers ran in from somewhere, grabbed the other guys who were there, talked about something in low voices, then the two ran off in different directions.

Just by looking, he could tell there was something going on.

And his gut convinced him it was nothing good.

"Wh-what is it?"

The semifer girl shrank in bewilderment. But Willem paid her no mind and grabbed onto the scruff of the neck of an orc who tried to rush past them.

"What happened?"

His question was short.

"Th-that's secret. Distribution of information can only be done through the proper channels."

"I want to thank you for all your honest, hard work, but—"

Willem glanced at the orc's rank. A foot soldier.

He showed him his own rank sewed onto his uniform.

"I am Second Enchantments Officer Willem Kmetsch. I am responsible for the management of dug weapons and the lepre—and the soldiers who wield them. Of course, I also have the right afforded my position to examine all the data regarding the current battle."

That was nothing but lies. Willem didn't even know how much power his position had in the first place. He had never been interested, so he never asked.

For now, he would simply push his luck.

"I request again that you disclose this information. *What happened?*"

With an empathic tone, he pressed closer.

The orc's shoulders shuddered in fear.

"We received contact from the first fleet. It was about the outcome of the battle on Island No. 15."

Willem's breath stopped.

Contact from the first fleet. The result of the fight on Island No. 15.

The one thing he was desperate to know.

Who had the advantage in the fight? When would it end? Were the girls still safe? The entire process had been hidden behind the veil that was the encampment. He and the others knew nothing. They weren't ready for anything.

What would happen to them?

"In our battle with Timere—"

Even if he did hear the end of that sentence—

The orc's face said everything.

That was why Willem smiled.

Because the inside of his heart was a mess.

He no longer knew how he would face the result he thought he was ready for, the outcome he had decided to accept.

So he smiled a weak smile, the corners of his mouth lifted just slightly.

He listened.

*   *   *

"—we have lost."

His vision went black.

His knees gave out, and he collapsed where he stood.

"A-are you all right?!"

The semifer girl rushed to him. But he could not even raise his head, much less take the hand held out for him.

What an idiot.

Somewhere in his heart, another version of himself scoffed.

It shouldn't have been a surprise. There was nothing that was supposed to be shocking.

Their chances of winning were just over half. He'd said that himself. He should have understood that they would lose in the case they couldn't reach 50 percent.

"Ha-ha, ha…"

His mouth was still twisted in a smile.

A laugh slipped so surprisingly easily from the back of his throat.

He could do nothing but laugh.

✝

"…I think we should send word soon."

"Of course! We have a Mr. So-and-so waiting for us with his heart pounding!"

"But…"

"Given the sssituation, I ssshall grant permissssion to ussse the communication crysssstal."

"See, even this important person is saying so!"

"But! People on the other end can see what we look like when we use the communication crystal!"

"Well, you know what this is for. Is there a problem?"

"I'm saying! We're covered in mud and not dressed very cute, and my hair is a mess!"

"Oh, you'll be fine just the way you are. By now, it isn't a relationship where there's any point in keeping up appearances, right?"

"But still, you know…"

"Because you haven't seen him in a few days?"

"Yes. I feel like I need to be ready."

✝

"…Huh…?"

Voices from somewhere.

They drew closer, accompanied by footsteps.

He lifted his head and looked in their direction.

"*Sigh*… Seeing up close the mind of a girl smitten is more annoying than I thought."

In an exaggerated manner, the girl with hair the color of withered grass shook her head in exasperation.

"That's not what it is! This is, like, a minimum of courtesy."

The girl with cerulean hair argued, her shoulders tensing.

"Your aloof appeal, which really took its time, by the way, is way too obvious again, y'know what I mean? It's like, what happened to the defiant Chtholly we had yesterday? I guess it is true that once a normally serious girl becomes conscious of boys, she becomes unruly, since she doesn't know her limits."

"Mm."

The girl with dull gray hair nodded shortly in agreement.

"Are you two siding against me?!"

The cerulean girl cried in pain.

The three of them somehow seemed exhausted. Their hair was mussed, their faces covered in mud and dust, and they wore tired linens on their bodies. This was obviously a time where it would be hard to say they looked stylish, even out of empty flattery.

And another thing. Something, at the very least, apparent from far away.

They were alive.

There were no visible wounds, either.

They moved; they talked.

"Oh." Ithea noticed the stare on her.

"Hmm?" Nephren tilted her head.

"Huh?" Chtholly turned around and froze.

"...*Yoooouuuuuu threeeee!*"

The darkness before his eyes was now dyed white.

While the fact that he still could not see anything had not changed, his body knew exactly what it needed to do.

—There was no need to bend his knees, to gather strength. He didn't have the time for that. He twisted his entire body and let it fall, as though slipping forward. Pushing himself forward with his legs, as animals were originally made to do, would always delay the initial movement. In the era when the emnetwiht fought with enemies who were far more powerful, they sought a technique that would let them run at a speed beyond their limits. Conceived at the ends of the north and studied in the battlefields to the west, it eventually crystallized. This technique, officially named the Nightingale Sweep, was difficult and would be mastered only by a small handful of adventurers and Quasi Braves. But for those who did, they gained a special move that could deceive even the elves' eyesight.

A summary of the result of activating this skill went something like, *That man, who'd just been relaxing his knees, without any preparation, dashed at a speed that did not even register to the eye.* Then—

"Wh-wh-wh-wh-wh-wh-what?! Wh-wha—?"

In the next moment, he held Chtholly, who should have been farther away, in a tight embrace.

"H-hey! Ow! That hurts! I can't breathe! Stop! I'm covered in mud and

I have scratches everywhere and I haven't cleaned myself and everyone is watching— Are you even listening?!"

Her words of protest, which she probably wasn't even aware of herself, of course never reached Willem's ears.

"...Where'd this guy come from?" Ithea asked the large lizardfolk man who stood beside her—Limeskin—but he merely shrugged slightly, giving no answer.

"I said we should have sent word earlier," Nephren muttered.

"You did say that, but did you think the officer would've been this broken?"

"Broken?"

"You know, doesn't this young man strike you as the type to put up a front, pretend he's all tough in an unnatural way? Or adopt a cynical attitude like a sourpuss? But then it's still kind of cute because neither really suits him?" Ithea drew circles in the air with her finger. "That's why I imagined a more chill reunion, where he just pats her on the head and says, 'Good job,' all somber-like, and then Chtholly gets all angry and says, 'Is that all you'll say to me?!' and stuff."

"...Willem has always been like this."

On the other hand, Nephren spoke smoothly, keeping Chtholly in the corner of her eye.

"He's hard-working, straightforward, and doesn't look at his surroundings very much. He doesn't stop until he's broken, and once he does stop, he doesn't move until he's fixed. It's risky and means he can't be left alone."

"Ahhh. I kinda get it, but I kinda don't." Ithea tilted her head in thought. "What do you think, Chtholly?"

"I think you need to stop chatting and help me out here!" she cried in protest.

"But I believe you should allow him to hug you until he's finished."

"No! Either my spine will snap or I'll suffocate or I'll absolutely die of embarrassment before that happens!"

"I don't think we need to worry about you suffocating if you're talking that much."

Nephren exhaled slightly, then tugged lightly on Willem's sleeve.

She stood on her toes and leaned in to his ear.

"It's okay. Everyone's here. We're not going anywhere," she whispered and patted him on the shoulder.

It seemed her words had an effect. Slowly, reason returned to Willem's eyes.

"...Ren."

"Mm-hmm." Nephren nodded slightly when he called her name.

"Ithea."

"Yup." She raised a hand.

"And"—he looked down to his arms—"Chtholly."

"Just hurry up and let me go. You're seriously embarrassing me!"

Once he glanced around and grasped what was going on, he murmured, "Sorry," and released her from his arms.

Chtholly stepped away silently and glared daggers at Willem, her face bright red—

"What a mess." Ithea grinned mischievously.

"Yes." Nephren nodded in defeat.

—and after a loud crack, Willem's cheeks burned.

Everyone,
in the Name
of Justice
-from dawn till dusk-

1. The Proper Use of Love and Justice

The ceiling in the strategy room was particularly high.

The desk placed in its center was rather large, and the chair, likely special ordered to match, had an excessively tall back. It was the result of having everything adjusted for those with the largest physiques, since this was a gathering place for soldiers of many races.

At the moment, the absurdly large lizardfolk—one of the largest—sat down in the sturdy chair made specifically for him, his throat rattling loudly with laughter. His expression was unchanging, which made his laughter feel rather creepy.

"The omen for Tiat's maturation as a faerie soldier... Bit early for that, no?"

Ithea tilted her head as she sat on the chair, swinging her feet freely.

The three of them had already bathed and cleaned themselves of dust and changed into the informal female guard uniform. It was strange how much more mature they seemed just by wearing clothes different from their casual outfits.

"I thought the little ones'd have at least two more years until they held a sword."

"You don't look too happy about that," Willem commented, his cheeks still red and swollen.

"Well, it ain't completely a good thing to go to the battlefield while they're young. There's a huge risk of accidental death, and they might end up weirdly traumatized even if it does go well. Honestly, I'm not sure how I feel about this."

"But we still have to wish her the best. You know that already, right? She's always been working her hardest to mature," Chtholly cut in from beside her.

"Well, sure, I know that, but…I just don't know how I feel!" The wrinkles between Ithea's eyebrows deepened.

"That's why I'm here. But anyway, tell me what happened in the end. I heard you lost in the battle at Island No. 15. So why is everyone here?"

Limeskin's laughter suddenly stopped, and his polished pebble–like eyes looked straight at Willem.

"I sssshall answwer your query, wounded warrior."

"O-okay…?"

Willem found himself flustered, not expecting him to respond to that, of all things.

"Firsst, allow me to praissse you. The blade you forged ssshone. It cssertainly crusshed the fangss of the beassst. Victory mosst cssertainly sshould have been oursss. However…opening beyond the sssigns of the augury wasss a trap. The fangss had coupled with a different ssset of fangsss. We sspared ourselvesss the recklessnesssss of facing unknown fangsss, sso we made the decssisssion to let the land fall."

…Uh?

"Sorry. I have no idea what you just said."

Even if Willem did, lizardfolk had a palate that was shaped differently from the other races, so their pronunciation was hard to understand. And Limeskin was also probably talking in his habitually roundabout way of speaking, so the difficulty of the conversation leaped up tenfold.

"I sssee."

Limeskin's shoulders dropped, deflated. It was typically an action he would find charming, but it didn't suit the massive lizard.

"Well, to sum it up, Timere'd tripped our tactical sensors, but it didn't seem like we'd be able to win against the Beast," Ithea piped up. She glanced at Chtholly before continuing. "This girl here seriously had some kind of power-up that I didn't really understand, so the initial phases of the battle were going super well. Seriously, what was that? I was honestly thinking at one point that we should just leave it all to her and have everyone else retreat."

"Seniorious, the most ancient of all holy swords, was even able to cut the Visitors. It won't lose to any other enemy as long as the right user uses it correctly—right?"

He touched on the subject, but Chtholly didn't answer, still turned away in a huff.

"She's a sulky one."

Ithea grinned. Willem interrupted by clearing his throat.

"...Anyway. You looked like you were winning, but you couldn't. What happened?"

"There was another that didn't set off the tactical sensors. Beast Six, Timere, is a monster you have to kill a whole handful of times for it to die in the first place. And on top of that, it gets stronger every time it sheds its shell after being killed. This time it was way bigger than usual, a huge monster that was still perfectly fine after we killed it more than two hundred times, and in the middle phases, it was desperate fight after desperate fight, even after Chtholly pushed beyond her limits. There was a lot of bad stuff already going on by that point..."

"But it was after the two hundred and seventeenth kill. *Two* of them came out of that shell."

"Huh?"

Out came a boneheaded voice.

"One of them was Timere, as it always had been. But the other was *something different.*

"The sensors can pick up all of Six's invasions, but there's no way they can detect something hitching a ride. It couldn't grow rapidly, unlike Timere, so it took time for it to come out. Almost none of the firearms worked against it, so we managed to narrow down which of the Seventeen Beasts it was, but otherwise, we didn't have a clue. We knew nothing, like what we should do first in order to fight successfully against it, not to mention not knowing if it was even an opponent we could fight and win against anyway.

"And so, we sent them both along with the island back down to the ground, then pulled out."

Well, that made sense. None of the Seventeen Beasts had wings, so they attacked via the very ineffective method of coincidentally drifting ashore. In which case, if there was a way to get them to go back to the surface, then it was possible to concentrate on fighting off the threat before them—

"—Seriously?"

"Seriously."

After losing the surface, all surviving life in the world had nowhere to call home but the floating islands.

In essence, the islands could be seen as all that was left of civilization. Losing one of them meant that this small universe grew even smaller.

"If we pushed Chtholly, and by that I mean putting her into overdrive, we might have won—lots of the lizard soldiers expressed that opinion. Mr. White Lizard here came to the conclusion that anything we tried in an unexpected battle would be a risk and that we couldn't discard our greatest strength for poor odds."

Limeskin, the white lizard in question, nodded.

"..."

For some reason, he glanced once at Chtholly from the corner of his eye.

"And sso, we have lossst."

Then, with an unreadable voice—which was normal, actually—he continued.

"Ressst easssy—it iss not sssomething for you to fret over. Everything in the ssky will fall one day. Moreover, life asss we know it hass not all come to an end. You being here may alssso be proof of that. We will be bussy from now on. May I leave the tassk of esssscorting thossse warriorss home to you?"

Limeskin glanced toward the three faeries.

"I guess...I don't mind."

He wanted to know what the soldier meant by, "We will be busy."

They probably wouldn't be able to recover the island that fell. There was grave meaning to this lost fight, and the responsibilities would be huge as well. There was probably much that he had to do as the commander. But now wasn't quite the time to ask about the things he wasn't speaking of himself.

So that was the full account of that long and dangerous battle.

"You did your best, you three." He gave his words of appreciation, regretfully thinking how that was all he could do.

Ithea giggled, Nephren tilted her head, and—

"Chtholly?"

—one girl was still looking away in a huff and did not even bother to glance in his direction.

"You are in quite the mood." Ithea shrugged, as though giving up on her.

"Are you okay with that?" Nephren asked, trying to catch a peek at her.

"…Shaddup." They were met with the quiet mutter of rejection.

When they left the strategy room, someone was waiting there.

There was a semifer girl, her sharp, pointed ears flattened in anxiety.

"Huh? You're that…" Before Willem could finish calling out to her, the girl turned her gaze to the one behind him.

"Uncle!" She raised her voice in delight.

He turned around slowly. Standing there was a giant lizardfolk.

"Uncle?" he confirmed.

"Mm." He nodded solemnly.

"You were a semifer? Your fur looks a lot like scales for one."

"No."

"Then is this kid actually a lizardfolk? Her scales look a lot like fur for one."

"No. Thissss girl iss the daughter of an old friend of mine. We have been clossse ssince ssshe wass little."

It was a pretty straightforward story, just as he thought might be the case.

"—What iss the matter, Phyr? Have I not told you to not sssshow your facssse in thesse partsss?" he reprimanded the girl with a rather strong tone.

"I came knowing I would be scolded. There is no one else I can trust besides you, Uncle," the girl answered in a flat, quiet voice.

Limeskin's eyebrow twitched, or so it looked like. He didn't have anything like eyebrows, of course.

"What happened?"

"A letter came. It said if we don't call off the ceremony, they will... assassinate Father."

Those were not peaceful-sounding words. Willem frowned.

"—Hmm."

"Father told me not to worry about it. He said it is just an empty threat and that the more we pay attention to it, the more confident they'll become. I do not think that is the case, however. Those *thugs* are not that soft. But not only has my father said as much, I cannot think of anyone else I can trust but you, Uncle."

"And sso hardsship followsss hardsship." The lizardfolk gazed up at the ceiling. "Phyr. I hate to sssay thiss, but I mussst be going."

"Uncle..." The semifer girl's expression clouded. There was a brief moment of silence.

"Willem. I have sssomething to asssk of you."

"I want to say no," he responded bluntly.

"...I have not sssaid anything yet."

"I can make a few guesses. Sorry, but I'm pretty busy with babysitting already."

He could hear Chtholly's mood souring behind him. She probably didn't like being treated like a child, but at the moment, he was going to pretend he didn't notice.

"I made up my mind a long time ago that I was gonna stay away from trouble involving women and children."

"That's not very convincing," Ithea muttered. She probably wanted to say that he was very much involved in the problem of the faerie soldiers despite whatever he said, but he was going to pretend he didn't hear that.

"I sssupposse it iss unavoidable... Sso, Chtholly. How iss your condition?"

"Huh?" Chtholly yelped wildly at hearing her name suddenly called. "Oh, yes. I am recovering. But I don't think I can use my weapon very well yet."

"I do not mind. Very well, I ssshall leave thiss girl'sss problem to you."

She blinked.

"Uh...um...well...I..." After a moment of exaggerated confusion, she closed her eyes and took in a deep breath. She then opened her eyes again. "B-but I'm a faerie. I don't know anything about this city, and I've never guarded anyone before, and I can't use my venenum right after such a long battle anyway..."

"However, it ssseemss there iss no one elssse to asssk. You will manage."

"That's... But..."

Chtholly threw a brief glance at Willem out of the corner of her eye.

It was clear what Limeskin was after. There was no need to ask Willem himself directly. If he forced an important job onto one of the faerie soldiers, then Willem would shoulder that responsibility in her place without a word. That was what he had discerned.

And though Willem loathed to admit it, the lizardfolk man was right on the money.

"...That's a low tactic. Where'd your warrior's pride go?"

"A warrior sshould alssso be honessst in victory."

That, too, was a rather loose interpretation of a warrior.

"I don't think I've ever had a conversation with you. Did I do something to make you hate me?"

"You have only given me interesssst in you."

"Erm, I would prefer this conversation to stay between my uncle and—"

The girl quietly tried to interject, but he interrupted her with a wave of his hand.

"No need for worry. While I do not yet know if thiss man can be depended on or trusssted, he will do the job."

"That's not a compliment."

"That wass not my intention."

Limeskin nodded slightly and began to walk off.

"I have left the ressst to you, Chtholly. Follow the ssignss of the wind with thosse who walk alongssside you and complete the misssssion."

"Uh...huh..."

In a partial daze, the remaining five watched him walk off.

"With those who walk alongside you," that damned lizard said.

Shut up, he thought. *You can't decide for me where I'll be walking.*

But he didn't say that. Had he responded like that, then it would be admitting that was his intention in the first place. He felt like they were way beyond the stage of admitting it or not after showing such disgraceful behavior, but there were still lines he would not cross.

"Um..."

A hesitant voice called out to him. Willem stopped her with his hand.

"Sorry, but I have a prior engagement. We'll walk and talk."

✝

After the rain, the old city was filled with a different flavor than he'd tasted yesterday.

The brick roads and the puddles glinted vividly, scattering the afternoon sunlight. The statues dotting the city were enveloped in a dim, out-of-focus light, and an air that conveyed an essence of holiness was wrapped around them.

Haaaah... He let out a big, shameless yawn. The clear, cool air filled his lungs and washed away the sleepiness that clung to the corners of his mind.

"There's a great feel about this town," Ithea said, stretching. "By the way, you think it's a good idea for us to just walk around the city like normal? Faeries are banned from wandering freely anywhere beyond Island No. 68, after all."

"You're on duty right now. The gracious first officer gave you direct orders."

"Well, that was just Chtholly. And strictly speaking, we're weapons, so while we can get direction on the battlefield, we can't officially accept missions."

"—Then, for appearances, it might mean you're under my command. That big lizard's scenario is probably, 'The first officer had to leave the site for unavoidable circumstances, so he transferred commanding rights to the second officer, who was on the premises'...or something."

"Huh. That's a pretty crafty story."

"It sure is. And he calls himself a warrior."

"Well, the second officer read up on his scenario pretty quickly, so I'd say he's about as good."

"That's unexpected. To say such a thing about this purehearted, good-natured young man."

"Ughhh, you have no shame."

Ithea cackled.

Willem chuckled, too—albeit a bit desperately.

His left arm was softly enveloped in a gentle warmth. He looked back to see Nephren, straight-faced, wrapped around it.

"Hey, Ren."

"Hmm."

"Can I ask you why you're clinging to me?"

"...Don't you feel calmer when you're warmer?"

The expression on his face looked as if to say, *"Why are you asking such an obvious question?"*

"Right now, you need body heat, Willem. My body temperature is higher than average, so it is most suitable." She spoke softly and gently, as though reasoning with a particularly dim child.

"I mean, I appreciate you being considerate and all, but..."

Even if he did, he wasn't so sure about the actions that came from it.

Thanks to Nephren's lack of curves, he managed to keep any strange thoughts at bay. He was a grown man, after all, and he was thankful for that.

He scratched his cheek with one of his free fingers.

"I'm fine, so let go. I don't think I can stand the stares we're getting anymore."

He could hear the giggles of the semifer passing them on the street. They probably saw the two featureless, Willem and Nephren, as close family members.

"…"

Nephren stared hard at Willem.

"You're still putting on a brave front a little. Not yet."

"It's this situation that's going to make me cry." His shoulders drooped. He was serious. "C'mon, Chtholly. Say something—"

He craned his head back.

Chtholly, who had been slowly trudging along, lifted her downward-cast gaze. She opened her mouth slightly. She searched for words but couldn't find them. Her face suddenly turned red, and she quickly looked away.

"A maiden's heart is a complicated thing," Ithea said, her voice troubled.

He almost blurted out, *"Maidens' hearts don't have a monopoly on being complicated!"* But in the end, he held his tongue. He couldn't tell if it was something he'd be made fun of if he said it out loud. And incidentally, it would be quite a while yet before Nephren, who seemed to be worried about him, would let go of his arm.

—Their sudden meeting after so long, along with his disgraceful behavior, had blown away so many other things. That was why he still hadn't said a single word of welcome to the girls, and he hadn't heard them announce their return.

Of course, it didn't feel like now was the time for that conversation.

(…Ooohhhh…)

It wasn't that he wanted a dramatic reunion scene.

He wasn't trying to say that he wasn't satisfied that he hadn't been able to greet the three in style.

He should just be pleased to confirm that they'd come back safely, and in reality, he wasn't unhappy with the result.

So, well…

He had to at least accept he would have a few uncomfortable thoughts. He knew that. He knew.

"Does it really look like I'm trying that hard?" he murmured, and Nephren's eyes wavered slightly.

"You really are alike," Ithea said suggestively and gave a small smile. Her expressions seemed strangely forced today.

He looked at her smile—and for some reason, that was what he felt.

✝

On the way, the semifer girl told them the story.

She called herself Phyracorlybia Dorio.

"Huh? Dorio? That means…"

"Yes. My father is Collina di Luce's current mayor."

She responded easily to Ithea's question.

Either due to her parents' upbringing or her natural disposition, her temperament was incredibly hard to read.

There was no way she was calm on the inside, after being rejected by the uncle she wanted to rely on and pushed onto a freakish group of people she didn't know. And yet, she gave no indication of bewilderment or irritation.

"Oh, I thought so."

The story was, the mayor of this town was originally a so-called upstart merchant who rose in the world in his lifetime, and Phyr (who herself asked to be called that, since her name was so long) was his daughter, who was born after he reached old age.

The city originally laid out the foundations for an aristocracy. It was only ten years prior that the mayoral system had been introduced. Because of that, there were quite a number of people who were not pleased with the current political system, with former nobles in the heart of it all. To them, having an upstart merchant as a mayor was an enemy of unforgivable appearance.

"Huh." He just brushed aside the explanation with a vague response.

"Then what was the letter you talked about earlier?"

Chtholly moved the conversation forward.

He thought she was being very earnest for someone who'd been named to take care of the whole situation.

"...It is a threat from one group to remove my father from his position and place a relative of the old nobility in the seat of mayor. They will do whatever it takes to oust him, as the one who is tarnishing the city's traditions and history."

"Ohh."

Another vague response.

It was a story he'd heard somewhere before—actually, the very one he'd heard just yesterday from that doctor. Judging by those gunshots that didn't suit such a quiet town, "*whatever it takes*" had a very broad range of meaning.

"At the end of next week, we will hold a ceremony to commemorate finishing construction on the Central Cathedral. My father is planning on speaking about the future this town should be heading toward there. A future that will open the doors to those of every race and will make this city into one of trade that will act as the bridge between islands. Most likely, they will use the Annihilation Knights, their agents, to attack. Then they may prepare to warn all of those who work with my father."

"...That sounds like the name of knights who get carried away by their youth and regret it five years later."

Oh, so Ithea thinks so, too. They were on the same page.

"It goes without saying that we plan to employ the minimum amount of security. However, considering the methods of the Annihilation Knights, I cannot imagine that would be enough. That is why I wished to ask for my uncle's—for First Officer Limeskin's help."

"What do you think?" he turned to his left arm and asked.

"No," Nephren responded bluntly. "In the end, the Winged Guard is an organization meant to fight against invaders from outside Regule Aire. They cannot meddle in the political affairs of every individual city. In the case that there is clearly an individual or a group that is trying to disrupt the peace, nearby Winged Guard soldiers are allowed to act in quelling it; however, that is ultimately for times of exceptional danger. Even if they know beforehand that there will be trouble, they cannot dispatch units ahead of time. That will be seen as interfering with political affairs."

"—What she said. The mayor probably knew that, so he likely didn't try to ask for help from that lizard himself."

"It can't be... Justice is clearly on our side! Why must restrictions be imposed on defeating the evil that harms the worlds of others?"

"*Justice* doesn't make it okay to use military force," he spat out abruptly. "It's the opposite. Justice is what's touted to justify the reasons for using military force. There will always be other reasons for wanting to pummel the enemy. Always. Because you want to take them away. Because you look down on them. Because you scorn them. Because you don't like them. Because you want them to disappear. Because you want to relieve stress. Or any combination of that." He waved his hand lightly, and like reciting an ancient poem, he spoke. "But no one wants to recognize any of that. At that point, you may as well beat the crap out of the other guy with no guilty conscience whatsoever. It's times like those people raise a flag under the name of justice to trick their enemies—and themselves. No one is aware of these things when they do that, so you get two people who wholly believe in their own justice fighting each other, and war starts. That's how it's always been."

"That's..."

Phyr fell silent.

—*What?* Willem thought.

The value of justice was determined by the persuasiveness to involve others and the strength of the belief of how deeply one could surrender oneself to it. It was meaningful enough if it was justice she could strongly believe in from the bottom of her heart. But she just could not mobilize the Winged Guard under that justice.

However, the justice Phyr touted wavered when people she'd just met today told her that, so he was a little disappointed.

"Well, you know. Even putting all that aside, the ceremony is next week, so we can't really keep you company. We have our own deal. Now we're going to the doctor's to pick up one of the kids, then in the evening, we'll get on an airship and fly home."

"Oh... I see." Phyr drooped her head.

"Wait up, wait up, just a second, Officer. I have two questions." Ithea tugged on his right sleeve.

"What?"

"What you said earlier, is that all right for the Brave who fought as the guardian of the great emnetwiht? Weren't you the face of justice at the time?"

"You think justice means shit in the struggle to survive? You space out for a second and you get wiped out, so I was just fighting back for my life. The will to survive is only an instinct, and when you start considering instinct and justice to be the same thing, then nothing in the world can ever be a crime."

"...I see. Regardless of the logic, I think I understand how you think, Officer." Ithea nodded slightly.

Nephren, who was still clinging to Willem's left arm, gripped slightly tighter.

"Another question. Why did you ask all that about the situation, only to be so rude to Miss Phyracorlybia? I feel like you've said gross things all cool-like, as if you can't leave a cute girl in distress alone."

"Don't call it gross."

Precisely because he wasn't completely unaware of that, it still hurt.

"I get it. Is it age? Women your age and older aren't women anymore or something?"

"Why does everything I do have to be so biased?" People had suspected him of that many times in the past, but it wasn't true. It shouldn't be. "That's not it. I just—"

"Just?"

Just—what?

Something he found hard to put into words coiled around the back of his throat.

"—Whoever it happens to be, I only want to be convinced of unconvincing things."

"Buh?"

Even he thought he'd said something he didn't quite understand. Sure enough, Ithea raised an eyebrow, making a strange face that was unbecoming of a girl her age.

"..."

For some reason, Nephren nodded slightly.

"Well, putting that aside, looks like we still have time until we need to go to the clinic."

It was hard to decide what to do with such an odd amount of time left. They didn't have enough time to take a preliminary look around the sights, and yet it would be a waste to spend it walking aimlessly.

—A delicious smell tickled his nose.

Willem turned his head as though he'd been jerked on a leash. He found a food stand set up on the back of a cart by the roadside. They were selling fried mutton and shredded potatoes wrapped in plentiful large, leafy vegetables. The titillating aroma of spices irresistibly aroused his appetite.

His stomach growled.

"Hey."

He turned around.

"Let's eat that. I haven't had breakfast yet."

"Ohhh, we should. All we've been eating is simple military provisions, so I'll welcome anything with strong flavor," Ithea murmured dully in agreement. Nephren didn't say anything, so she probably wasn't against it. And just as Chtholly was about to say something—

"—Please wait."

There came a weak yet sharp voice.

For a moment, he truly didn't know who was talking. He slowly turned around, feeling something cold down his spine. There, somewhat unexpectedly but also naturally, was the figure of someone he didn't expect.

Phyracorlybia Dorio.

Though he was looking straight at her, his instinct doubted if that was really her. The presence around her was completely different from what it was a few moments ago. He just could not believe it was the same person.

"The spices are clearly much too strong, and their certificate of authorization is not posted on the front. That is, without a doubt, a shop that is feeding people shoddy meat that is barely legal."

"O-oh."

Her tone was unusually strong.

Willem unwittingly recoiled, overwhelmed.

"And it is more expensive than market price. Even locals clearly know it looks off; tourists buy and eat it without knowing and presume it to be normal. If these practices continue, it is clear that the city itself will lose trust. No matter how much my father sues them, those hooligans refuse to disappear."

There was a dangerous light glinting in her eye.

Her body wavered like a specter.

"Come this way," she said while starting to walk off.

"H-hey!"

"Were you to eat there, then that shoddy taste will become your memory of dining in Collina di Luce. As long as I am with you, I cannot allow such a thing. It would be tantamount to shaming my uncle. Come with me. You will see real Collina di Luce–style wrapped lamb."

She took brisk, wide steps and turned onto a back street.

"…I'm surprised," Nephren murmured in a voice contradicting that very statement. "She left. What do we do?"

"No matter what, it doesn't really feel like we have a choice, does it?"

"We woke the sleeping dog, so I guess we gotta tag along… Chtholly?"

The girl practically jumped when she looked up from her feet at her name suddenly being called.

"Uh… Wh-what?"

"Are you doing okay? You've been silent as a statue this entire time—"

"That is pretty quiet," Ithea interrupted.

"If you're still tired, then you should say something. I don't feel like pushing you in a place that's not a battlefield."

"No, that's not it…" She shook her head slowly. "I'm sorry I worried you."

It seemed like she'd calmed her anger, but she was still acting weird.

"If you're telling me you've still got pools of activated venenum in your body, then I could *ease* it for you, like last time?" he suggested, cracking his knuckles.

"Ease—" Chtholly stared absently at Willem's face, and after a moment, her cheeks suddenly turned bright red. "—No! I don't! If you did *that*, then I probably wouldn't ever be able to stand up!" she said as she flailed both her arms about.

"What do you mean by *ease*?"

"Hey! Stop getting curious about this!"

"Well, if that's how you're going to respond, then it's pretty much impossible to not be curious, right? Is it like, there's something you really want to talk about so you're asking us in a roundabout way to catch up?"

"Listen to me! It's nothing, I swear, and besides, nothing happened!"

"You know, I kind of like how you dig your own grave deeper the more you talk. You'll burrow straight to the bottom of the island at this rate. It's okay."

"Listen!"

The moment Chtholly raised her voice even louder in argument—

"Um?"

A small voice, chill as a blade, cut in from beside them.

They turned around. There stood a lone semifer girl, standing at the entrance to the alleyway, a ghastly air about her.

"—Did I not ask you to follow me?"

"Apologies! We're coming now!"

They jumped forward into the alley, and all of them followed Phyr.

She led them to a cozy butcher shop nestled in the corner of a small plaza.

"No stalls?"

"Of course, there are many good stalls, but if you're simply looking for a cheap and delicious wrapped lamb at this time in this neighborhood, then I cannot give any other answer than this. All the locals, even five-year-old children, know of this place."

"You have some smart five-year-olds."

They paid the silent ballman shop owner and received one—*wrapped lamb, was it?*—a full size bigger than the ones they saw at the stall earlier.

He bit into it.

"This is delicious."

"Isn't it?"

Phyr sniffed proudly.

"The sharp-tasting spices are subdued, and instead there are more acidic herbs mixed in. I see—I could eat all this without trouble with seasoning like this."

"Right? Right?"

After bobbing her head up and down several times in a nod, Phyr faced the ballman butcher and gave him a thumbs-up. He, too, gave a thumbs-up right back.

(...Hmm?)

He felt an uncomfortable prickling on the back of his neck. The faint sensation of malice and animosity.

Those rumored Whatever Knights again, huh, he thought. But it was a different breed from what he felt yesterday when they first arrived in town. It was vague then, who that animosity was meant for, but this time—

"—Hey, Phyracorlybia."

"I said earlier that you may call me Phyr."

"Right. Hey, Phyr. Do you like this city?"

Her eyelids quickly traveled down and up her large eyes.

"What is this, all of a sudden?"

"Just answer. So?"

A short moment passed.

"Yes. I think there is no better city."

"Is it because of the four-hundred-year-plus history? Or because it's the most prominent metropolis? Or because industry is thriving? Or because the food's good?"

"Your queries are quite spiteful, aren't they?"

"I get that a lot."

Willem cackled as he took another bite of the wrapped lamb.

"…Everything you mentioned now is, without a doubt, an indispensable part of this city's charm. They all shine vividly within my heart. However, I do not think any of them have…penetrated its core."

"I see."

It seemed like the vegetable used for the wrapping was also done up in a special way. The flavor changed ever so slightly with every bite. As he was chasing those transitions with his tongue, he suddenly found that there was nothing left in his hands.

Even though he'd somehow just managed to put all that away in his stomach, he still wanted another bite. Now that was the real Collina di Luce–style wrapped lamb. He understood well why Phyr had insisted on this place.

"…I know of no city besides this one." The girl in question responded, carefully choosing her words. "This is my precious hometown and the entirety of my world as I know it. That is why I love this city, as though I would love the whole world."

"That's an embarrassing thing to say."

"And who made me say it?!" Her face flushed (though it was hard to tell over her fur), and she argued. "You are truly a spiteful man. Do you enjoy exposing my most intimate thoughts?!"

"Sure. I'm not gonna deny that's how I feel," Willem said, licking the grease off his fingers. "I ate good food from this city. I saw the face of some-one who likes it here. Now I feel more like doing something for this place, more than when you were blabbering on about justice."

He glanced at her startled expression out of the corner of his eye.

"And what on earth is that supposed to mean?"

"Exactly what I said... But let's put that aside for now. I'm here and may as well. If you're free after this, you think you could do a little thing for me?"

"...What is it?"

Phyr, unsure of his true intentions, looked at him suspiciously, and Willem grinned back.

"Could you show us around town a little later?"

†

"I—I wasn't scared or hurt or anything, okay!"

Those words of insistence were the very first out of Tiat's mouth, her eyes welling up with tears.

"There weren't any shots or anything, at all!"

"I know, I know."

After receiving a light pat on the head, she gave a small hiccup.

"She's perseverant, honest, and straightforward. She'll be an excellent soldier."

The stern-faced cyclops gave his seal of approval with a gentle smile. Ignoring that first half, Willem thought it was a strange evaluation, unsure if he should be happy or sad about the latter half.

"Those behind you... You're girls who were adjusted here before. I'm glad to see you're well."

That was meant for Chtholly and the others.

"It has been a long time since we last saw you. Thanks to you, we are managing to fight well."

Chtholly alone bowed her head reverently. Ithea just cackled vaguely, and Nephren wore her usual composed expression, not showing any response.

The doctor must have noticed something strange about those responses.

"Could it be, you—?"

"Whoops, let's not say any more than that, Doc."

Ithea quickly cut off the cyclops doctor as he began to speak.

"Oh, so you guys *are* hiding something."

"Tsk-tsk-tsk, you should not be sticking your neck into girls' affairs, Officer. Keeping a proper distance is the first step in keeping both parties happy."

"You think so?"

Willem gave up on trying to get it out of Ithea, who was clearly trying to deceive him, so he directed his attack at the doctor. But the cyclops just scratched his cheek and responded with a troubled look, "I shouldn't be the one to tell you," and didn't elaborate further.

"As for what I do wish of you, well… Keep a careful watch over these children."

As the faerie warehouse manager, it was in Willem Kmetsch's job description to watch over the faeries anyway. At the very least, that's what Willem himself thought.

So he didn't need to be told outright; he was planning on doing that from the very beginning.

When he gave his response—

"Okay."

With a quiet expression, the cyclops nodded.

It bothered him a little why Ithea was looking at the cyclops with such a rueful expression.

In order to get home to Island No. 68 from here, they would have to take a good number of airship transfers. And there was only a small number that ran every day. To add to that, it was, of course, not a distance where the faeries could easily fly them home.

Therefore, until the airship they were aiming for left in the evening, whatever they ended up doing, they couldn't leave Collina di Luce.

"And so, we will use this time to sightsee this city!"

Willem proclaimed proudly before the other five—the faeries, who had changed back to regular clothes, and Phyr.

"Huh?" Chtholly murmured with a serious expression.

"Hmm?" Ithea looked as though she didn't quite believe what he said.

"Oh." Nephren's eyes, for once, glimmered with delight.

"…" Phyr said nothing, her gaze downward.

"Yaaaaaaaaaay!" Tiat clapped her hands as hard as she could.

"This is for you, since you can never move around freely outside the island, and you never get opportunities like this. This is right after a well-fought battle; you won't get in trouble if you cut loose a little."

"Wait, wait. What should we do with our dug weapons?"

Ithea lightly waved the large wrapped package—a swathed enchanted longsword—that was strapped to her back.

"I really hope you're not gonna make us walk around with this heavy stuff on our backs."

"Leave it at the clinic. We'll just pick it up on our way back."

"They're very expensive and important and precious secret weapons, you know…"

"That's why we leave them with people who know their value. They're not something those luggage thieves want anyway, so don't worry."

"I suppose so."

"Mm. I am glad that we will be able to see some things. But…" Nephren peered at Phyr's face. "Phyr, are you okay with this?"

It wasn't too long ago that they'd coldly refused to do what Phyr had asked of them. She probably wasn't too delighted to be asked of something so frivolous right afterward.

"You have no more reason to come with us."

"I have no choice." Phyr sighed briefly. "You have already heard of one of the dark sides of the city. If you left as you are now, you may mistake the city as one of violence and schemes. And that is right after I asked such a heedless favor of you."

As she spoke, the force in her voice grew stronger and stronger.

She clenched her fist tightly before her chest, and bright flames burned in her large eyes.

"Uhhh, hello? Phyr? Miss Phyr?"

"I cannot stand such a thing. Therefore, I have no choice but to have you understand the appeal of this city through my actions alone. Starting now, I will work my absolute hardest to show you around this wonderful city today."

Everyone's gazes gathered on Willem.

"...What?"

"What did you do to her? What ideas did you put into her when we were eating just now?"

"Hey, c'mon, that makes me sound bad. I just gave her appropriate advice and asked a favor."

"Ohhh, so you tricked her with your smooth talk."

And he'd *just* told Ithea to stop making him sound bad.

The city of Collina di Luce was huge.

Just moving around to take a look at all the famous sightseeing spots would take more than a day, several days if one decided to add museums and art galleries to their route.

Since they had only about half a day to sightsee, it was crucial that they decide which landmarks they could visit and choose the most efficient mode of transport. In both cases, they needed the help of someone who was intimately familiar with the city.

And so, they asked Phyr to come along and show them around—

At least, *that much of the story was true.*

So, well.

They could leave the rest of the story for later.

2. The Incorrect Use of Love and Justice

They saw something called the Perjurer's Grave.

It was apparently the grave of a legendary swindler who had run amok two hundred years ago. The headstone, which was erected through the donations of those he'd tricked in his lifetime, for some reason read, HERE LIES AN HONEST MAN.

Just how on earth did that happen? It had brought about various theories and speculation, developed into its own genre called "The Perjurer," and led to a brief boom in Collina di Luce's rumor mill.

"I favor the legend that he murmured words of true love at the very end. Though I only believe it insofar as I hope that was what actually happened."

"For me it's gotta be the legend where he exposed the lies of corrupt nobles, showing them all that they were no match for him when it came to lying. That's just a plain cool story."

"—There's the tale that said he angered the Poteau gods, who cursed him so all his lies would become truths. That was interesting."

Huh. Looks like there really are lots of theories.

Well, in the end, that was what it was like for a past that no one knew the truth of. The truth was fabricated to suit someone's needs or shaped in a way that was the most interesting or odd, and that tale took the place of the truth.

Everyone believed the stories they wanted to believe. That was fine as long as it didn't cause problems. The world would still keep on spinning smoothly.

They saw something called the Lovers' Staircase.

The story behind it was clear. It was a romance between a noble girl, who hated her arranged marriage and ran away from home, and a scoundrel of a young man, who made his living through petty thievery.

It was here, where they bumped into each other and rolled down the steps, that they met by chance and became aware of each other.

At the top and bottom of the staircase stood a huge sign, spoiling the scenery. On it was the emblem of the city council and a brief warning: NO ROLLING.

"No rolling?!"

Tiat wailed like it was the end of the world, inviting the soft chuckles of passersby. They likely often heard very similar-sounding whining.

He would pretend he never noticed Chtholly's shoulders silently sagging.

"Hey, hey, Officer."

A tug on his sleeve.

"I know you're acting more and more normal, but could you, like, say something a little nicer to Chtholly?"

There was the cerulean-haired faerie, avoiding his gaze.

"She's pouting right now, but she was really working hard up till yesterday."

"I know that, but I've never been good at dealing with girls in bad moods."

"You really look like you are, but you're the only one who can fix her mood, Officer."

With a quick motion, he ruffled Ithea's unruly hair. "Bwuh?!" She jumped with more energy than he thought she would. "Wh-what was that, all of a sudden?!"

"Nothing, just thought you were a good kid, and I wanted to praise you. You put your friend first, even though you work hard and feel just as tired yourself."

"Don't worry about me! We're talking about Chtholly now!"

Unusually for Ithea, her face went red as she swatted away his hand. He understood that she wasn't used to being complimented, but he thought absently that her reactions were excessive.

—There was a slight uncomfortable prickling at the back of his neck.

The distance between them and the presence of their pursuer widened slightly, but instead, their numbers grew.

"Should be time to fish 'em out soon, huh…?"

"Hmm, what'd you say?"

Ithea responded to his muttering, and he placed his open palm on her head (and she gave a cry of "Gyaah!"), then called out to Phyr, who walked in front of them.

"Can I make a request for the next place? I wanna go somewhere that's secluded, where tourists rarely ever go."

"Oh, is that a challenge for the tour guide?"

Tossing aside the expression of a fragile young lady, Phyr smiled defiantly.

"Here is the Wishing Well."

She pointed to a small plaza, the intersection of six small alleyways. In the middle sat a plain-looking well, with nothing in particular to make it stand out.

"While it's not as widely known as the Central Cathedral or Barley Square, where you'll find ten out of ten people who know about it, it has been used countless times in projections, so those who know it, know it."

Tiat was nodding her head up and down vigorously.

"When you say *wishing*, you mean throw a coin in and make a wish?" Ithea asked, peeking inside the well. "That's so romantic, like a fairy tale!"

"Unfortunately, not everyone's wishes will come true. There certainly is a spirit that lives in the well, and it actually has the power of Realization, but they say it can only grant the wishes of every thousand or ten thousand people who throw in copper coins."

"Man, when you put it in numbers like that, we lose the fairy-tale feeling pretty fast."

"On the other hand, one person can throw in as many coins as one likes. Since the chances of success go up according to the value of the coins tossed in, some people who earnestly want their wishes to come true bring entire bags of twenty-bradal coins."

"…And now the feeling of romance is gone, too."

"Did you know it was illegal to use this well for a while? It was about fifty years ago, during the gambling prohibition era, because the chances were much too high."

"I don't need to hear any more. Something inside me feels like it's about to shatter."

As those two chatted, Tiat grabbed a coin with her small hand, struck a pose, then threw it into the well.

She apparently didn't have any particular wishes she wanted to come true but instead just wanted to copy the scenes she'd always dreamed about from the projection house. Ithea hugged her tightly as she squirmed, saying, "Yes, that's right! That's how you seek out romance! Awww, you're so cute!"

Beside them, Nephren quietly threw a coin in with the same pose. It looked like she had her own thoughts about this place. There came the quiet *plop* of water.

Someone was missing.

When that crossed his mind, he whirled his head around and found the last person all too quickly. Chtholly Nota Seniorious stood a short distance away from the well, alone.

"Aren't you gonna try it?"

He approached her, sitting down on a stack of crates piled next to her.

"No. I don't feel like making any wishes."

Her voice was quiet, her eyes still turned away sullenly.

"Really? That's a surprise. I thought you'd like stuff like this."

"Well, I guess I don't hate it, and if I had to choose, I'd say I love it..." Her words came out somewhat muddled, and she faltered. "But I really don't feel like it.

"...That stuff is probably for people who haven't met their goal yet, who do it to reaffirm their resolve inside themselves. It leaves a scar on their wallet, and that scar is a reminder of the price of their resolve. That's why it doesn't resonate with people who've lost sight of their goal or people who instead feel like they can reach it on their own."

Her intonation was strange—somewhat sad, somewhat kind, somewhat of neither.

"Hey. Are you really doing okay? You're acting kind of weird today."

"I told you—I'm fine. Girls have days they want to soak in ennui for no reason, you know."

Ahh, sounds a little like the usual Chtholly. That's a relief.

That relief pushed him forward, and he felt like putting the things he usually swallowed into words.

"…I want to thank you."

"Huh?"

Chtholly was honestly surprised by his words.

"All I thought about was dying. All I ever wanted was to go to all the people who were waiting for me to come home. Since meeting you guys, I've changed a little. Now I think about wanting a place to call home. Since meeting you, I've been saved a little. Now I think about how I can wait for someone, too. And even still, since you came home, I'm now, well…a little happier."

"Huh?"

She's seriously weirded out by this.

"Wait, don't back away so much! Don't make a face like I'm some embarrassing creature! I haven't even said anything weird."

"All of it was weird. Especially how you said all those embarrassing things with a straight face."

"What, you want me to say them with a big grin on my face?"

"That isn't the question, but…"

Chtholly smiled.

It was calm, happy, joyous, clear…and somehow empty.

For a moment, Willem's heart skipped a beat.

"What you said was embarrassing, but you telling me that does make me happy, yeah. I feel like there is a reason for living as long as I've made someone happy. Mm. I suppose I didn't choose the one I love incorrectly."

…Oh.

In a fluster, Willem peeled his gaze from Chtholly's profile.

Oh no. What was that? What was that smile?

She's a kid. At least for now. He repeated that to himself. He shouldn't take the word *love* seriously. He couldn't honestly accept a child's affection. Even if he did, it would just bring her unhappiness later. *Right*, he repeated to himself in his mind.

There was a mysterious allure to Chtholly's expression and words that would not leave him in a calm state of mind if he didn't.

(...*Right.*)

This girl is looking straight at me— So Willem realized. That was why her words, at times, moved his heart head-on.

He wouldn't be able to brush it off like it was just a child's first crush or a momentary trick of the mind anymore.

"What's that response supposed to mean?"

Chtholly chuckled softly.

Nothing—he somehow managed to swallow that cheap response.

"You're makin' me blush. That bad?"

"Not at all. It's great."

The girl laughed out loud.

For some reason, she seemed like she would burst into tears behind that smile.

This was bad. It now felt like a situation he wasn't good at dealing with. He was now looking at Chtholly, who should have been a child, as a woman.

Willem wasn't good at dealing with women.

He had absolutely no clue how he should read them, how he should take every single word, every single action.

That was true even for people like Nygglatho, who were the sort of characters who were easy to read. There was absolutely nothing he could say about people like this girl now, who hid things behind smiles.

Nevertheless, he couldn't just stay quiet about it. After all was said and done, he was still dealing with Chtholly, so he should come out firmly and force his way. Just as he took the plunge and opened his mouth—

"Sorry to interrupt your fun outing, ladies."

He heard the oddly clammy voice of a man.

"Friends?"

Tiat looked up to Phyr and asked, but Phyr shook her head.

"No. I do not recognize them…"

"But of course. This is our first meeting together."

The speaker was a cat semifer who wore a strangely crisp suit (he didn't wear it too well), and five younger men stood behind him. They were also all semifer, and while their faces and clothes varied, what they had in common was how unrefined they looked, and they all wore copper-colored bandannas wrapped around their wrists.

"We're surrounded."

Nephren murmured to herself quietly while Phyr looked around in a panic. Interesting—at some point, two or three youngsters had appeared out from each of the alleyways that extended from the small plaza and positioned themselves there. They were all semifer, and all wore bandannas around their wrists.

And they couldn't find anyone else in the plaza besides them. It wasn't a very populous place to begin with, or maybe that was the very reason why. He even got the impression that it was only this corner of town that had been cut away and closed off.

"No…"

"We don't want to do this the *haaard* way. Lady Phyracorlybia. If you want to keep your dirty featureless friends safe, then I hope you would be so kind as to take us up on our invi*taaa*tion."

There was a rather sticky quality to his voice. He was trying to speak theatrically—and failing. Though it was obviously his best attempt at acting smug, it was clearly not his strong suit, leaving only unnatural buffoonery.

That about sums it up. Not that I care.

"Tell me who you are!"

Phyr was trying to act brave, but her voice shook.

"Heh-heh, it's not something we *hiiide*, but since you bothered to *aaask*, I think we will take the liberty to—"

"The Annihilation Knights, right?"

Every pair of eyes turned to Willem.

Their gazes still trained on him, Willem reached down to his feet and collected a few pebbles. One by one, he lightly tossed them into the air and caught them with the same hand.

As he played with them, he called out, "Hey, Phyr."

"Uh, ah, yes? What is it?"

"I bet you haven't been outside your home alone very much lately, have you?"

"Huh? Y-yes. Father told me I shouldn't go out for a while."

"But you just had to ask a favor from that big white lizard, so today you left the house in secret. That right?"

"Yes… But why do you…?"

"To sum it up, these Knights were after the mayor's daughter to use as a bargaining chip in negotiations with him. To be more precise, they plan to negotiate with their sponsor by offering him that bargaining chip."

Anxiety rippled through the group of semifer.

"You were just lucky that they didn't find you in the time between when you left the house and when you found us. And so that probably means that they're unlucky they found you with us."

Tiat stared wide-eyed, Nephren wore a blank expression, Ithea murmured "Ohhh" in understanding, and Chtholly's face read, *"Here we go again."*

"They've been watching us intently ever since we ate. It felt like they were in a big hurry to gather support, so after walking awhile in obvious places, I decided to move somewhere without anyone else around. And just as I predicted, these punks decided to show their faces."

"W-wait a moment. I have no idea what you're talking about. The way you speak almost sounds like—"

"Yup. Used you as bait. I wanted to have a little chat with these guys."

At a loss for words, Phyr stood there frozen in shock.

"Chaaat?" the suited semifer interjected, his tone suspicious. "You seem pretty proud of how fast your brain and mouth move, *frieeend*. We didn't exactly come here to have a *chaat*—"

"Ithea."

Interrupting his statement, Willem called out to the girl standing next to Phyr.

"What is it?"

"I heard the great leaders of these Knights don't have any understanding of Sight. Show 'em a bit of what fully activated venenum looks like."

"Hmm—you want me to go all out?"

"No. Don't do anything more than show."

"Understood, Officer Scoundrel."

There was a bright flash of light.

She lifted her head, as though looking up to the sky, her eyes closed, and sprouting from her back, huge wings the color of wheat unfurled. They were purely phantasm wings, made just from light.

But because they were nothing but a phantasm, they could easily break the chains of the land, even without fluttering and stirring the wind.

"Wow…"

Phyr had likely heard that Ithea and the others were nothing but Guard personnel, so a voice of admiration and surprise slipped absentmindedly from her lips.

"…So you can use venenum. Not every day you see someone with the power to make wings. This means you can easily escape from a crowd this big, *riiight*?"

The suited semifer narrowed his eyes.

Judging by how his eyes darted around, he probably had a plan for dealing with an opponent who tried to escape via the skies. In all likelihood, it was probably a gunpowder weapon.

But in a situation like this, where a personal firearm had relatively poor handling, low accuracy, and a short range, their opponent would have a hard time suppressing them. Not only that, but a misfire that hurt Phyr would not mean good news for these thugs.

"Guess that makes things easier for us."

Willem surmised that they wouldn't be doing anything reckless anymore. And that didn't seem like a mistake.

"If what you said earlier is true, that means you inviting us here means you prepared all this. Then you should be ready for that much. How*eeeever*, what is it you want to talk about after all this?"

"Hmm, well, it's not that important," he started with a little disclaimer. "Do you all like this city?" he asked.

—The wind blew through the plaza.

Clumped scraps of paper rustled and rolled along the brick road.

There came the faint sound of an animal howling from far away.

Tiat's eyes glazed over, no longer able to understand the situation.

Nephren, surprisingly, put her hand to her mouth, smiling slightly.

Ithea, still floating in the air, shook her head in exasperation.

Chtholly, still looking away in a huff, muttered, "I suppose I did choose the one I love incorrectly," which he couldn't just ignore—actually, he should be happy about it.

Phyr's round eyes rounded even more, and all the remaining semifer stayed quiet, unsure how to respond.

"…What is this, all of a sudden?"

After a little while, the suited semifer, acting as representative for their questions, asked.

"Just answer. Well?"

A short beat.

"Of *cooourse*, the answer is *ooo*bvious."

"Hmm. Is it because of the four-hundred-year-plus history? Or because it's the most prominent metropolis? Or because industry is thriving? Or because the food's good?"

"What a stupid question. What sort of answer is possible, besides all that which is right? Collina di Luce is the very jewel box of the heavens. It is the capital of our pride, polished over the ages, and holds all the virtues any city could possibly have—"

"—And are those the words of your sponsor?"

His statement suddenly stopped.

"How much do you really know?"

"Nah, that was just a leading question. But thanks to that, you confirmed some things for me." He sighed a long sigh. "Your actions are way too inconsistent. To start, threatening to assassinate the mayor at the ceremony is incredibly stupid. If your goal is to have your demands met, then you shouldn't rely on assassination. If your goal is the assassination itself, you shouldn't send a threat. Even if you wanted to scare the mayor's supporters by announcing it before killing him, then you shouldn't have specified the ceremony. With overwhelming finances and executive skills, succeeding in the assassination even after forcing past tight security at the ceremony would have serious appeal. But then the mayor and his faction would be thoroughly prepared to fight back.

"So why did you send the letter? I'm guessing something like childish vanity, typical of gaudy nobles."

Well, if that was all, then that was already made clear by how they seriously called themselves the Annihilation Knights.

He stopped talking for a moment, but no one said anything. They were waiting for Willem's next words.

"On the other hand, your skills shouldn't be that bad, considering how fast you gathered this many people after finding us. And kidnapping the mayor's daughter is realistic. You'd discover after a little investigation that she's kind of ignorant and a naive woman. Plus, the person who thought of the kidnapping and the person who sent the threat are two different people. No matter how you think about it, doing it the other way around would have been way more successful. Not doing that means you never had the option. You were probably forced to carry out an unreasonable assassination, making you panic, then planned an almost arbitrary kidnapping. Well, that's how I see it; I didn't do anything but ask some leading questions and check my answers against yours. For now, I'm just glad I was right."

He said it all in one go, then nodded a few times to himself.

"...What do you want?"

The suited semifer's tone of voice changed.

"Hmm?"

"There's no reason for you to blab about your tricks here if you were just going to beat us up. You've shown your hand, which means now you plan to negotiate?"

"Great. I like it when people make things easy for me." Willem clapped his knee and stood from the crate. "Let me get straight to the point. Sell out your sponsor. The way I see it, you don't care about the mayor or whatever. You're just foot soldiers, acting on the ideas of your employer. Not only that, but you're fed up with your airheaded boss forcing you to do unnecessary work. I'm sure there are some of you who think it's about time to just give up."

Several of the semifer men visibly reeled.

One of them reached into his pocket. When he pulled out his hand, he was gripping a gun. He was about to aim it at Willem with dexterous speed, but he gave a cry and dropped his crucial weapon.

The small pebble that had struck the back of his hand dropped to the ground and rolled away.

"By the way, your bodies themselves will be collateral for this deal. Whether or not you'll get out of this unharmed depends on your attitude."

Willem informed them in a low voice, keeping his stance from throwing the pebble.

He hadn't used any magic or anything. He'd simply tossed the piece of gravel but, in doing so, caught everyone off guard. It was like a little magic trick that wouldn't work on people who knew about it, but for that reason alone, it made those who didn't know the *trick* feel like a spell had been cast on them.

"Well?"

✝

It was all pretty quick after that.

The semifer swallowed Willem's idea easily, and they gave the name of the former noble who was their client. On top of that, they said they would also sell out proof that he ordered quite a few antisocial actions, so they said they would bring that directly to negotiations with the mayor.

The entirety of the Annihilation Knights most likely weren't all gathered there in that alley, but they probably wouldn't be acting out as much as they had been before, now that they were down a leader and a dozen members.

At the very least, they probably didn't have to worry about any assassination taking place at that ceremony.

And so, Limeskin's orders had been executed successfully, but—

Willem's cheeks burned.

He thought absently about how hard this day had been on his cheeks.

"I really do hate you."

Phyr lamented, holding her red and swollen palm to her chest, her eyes brimming with tears.

"I understand that you did this for me. However, I cannot accept that you chose such a manner to accomplish it—"

He thought so.

This young lady was straightforward, meek, hardworking, honest, and much too principled. And probably the type to ask the same of the person in front of her. *Foul play* was a term that didn't have a space in her mind, and she would probably fall into a panic if she was set up, never mind if she needed to set up a trap herself.

"Y-you even touched my stomach when we first met…"

"Huh?"

"Do not tell me you don't know! To show one's stomach is to devote oneself completely to lycanthropes! One does not even expose it to close family members!"

How the hell was I supposed to know that rule? Are you actual dogs or what?!

…But she probably wouldn't believe him if he yelled that. "U-uh-huh." He made a boneheaded noise and looked away. That made sense; now he understood the context of the "blade" that she'd mentioned then. He learned something new. Next time he would have to be more careful.

"Well, see. I'm sorry for a lot of things. I won't ask you to forgive me, but at least let me apologize."

Phyr groaned.

"It was exactly as Uncle said. Expectations and hope aside, I cannot depend on or trust you."

"Rgh."

He faltered. He hated how he had nothing to say back.

"—Now, I feel slightly relieved. I will accept your words of apology. But do not take it the wrong way, since I still loathe you."

"Yeah. Of course, that's fine." Willem nodded and whirled around to face what was behind him. "Okay, guys, it's almost time to go…back…home…"

His voice grew quieter, and he was almost inaudible by the end.

Frigid stares were pointed mercilessly at Willem.

"Sure. Let's go."

Chtholly was looking at him with narrowed eyes and a clammy gaze.

"I thought I knew you were this kind of person, Officer, but now I don't know…"

Ithea still beamed brightly, but her mouth was drawn taut.

"Let's hurry. They will stop selling airship tickets soon."

Nephren spoke lightly as usual, but her voice was somehow cold.

"But I wanted to see more!!"

And then there was Tiat, who was upset about something else entirely.

While all four of them were different, there was no mistake that they were all mad about something.

"Why did you choose such a dangerous way to do it?"

The group made their way back to the clinic to pick up their dug weapons.

It was Chtholly who asked that on the way.

"Hmm?"

So she was talking to him. She was probably in a better mood now.

"There were so many other safer options than purposefully luring them into a deserted place, weren't there? Is it because you wanted to show off or for some other stupid reason like that?"

"Oh, no. I just wasn't very confident. I was talking like I'd inferred everything then, but all that was assumptions based on experience. I recalled past cases where people acted in a similar pattern to these guys, then thought about what had been going on behind the scenes in those times. Then I just filled in the details as I watched their reactions. That's why it was ideal to make it a situation where it seemed like we were feeling out each other's intentions."

"Based on experience...? What kind of life teaches you how to do that?"

"Well, it was a dangerous time. Working as a Quasi Brave meant I got wrapped up in some sort of power struggle at least once a month. Thanks to that, by the end, I could dodge a knife in my sleep, detect poisoned food on instincts alone. Pros use poison that has no smell or taste, so you can't rely on your nose or tongue."

He cackled cheerfully.

"...Is that supposed to be funny?"

"It's because I'm alive somehow. I wouldn't be able to laugh if I were dead."

Chtholly frowned. He'd been somewhat confident with that joke, but it looked like it was a complete misfire.

"All right, I'll admit it wasn't a great way to do it. But I figured you'd activate your venenum the moment you noticed something was wrong, and that's exactly what happened. But you guys just finished a long battle. I shouldn't have gone along with a plan that made you use your venenum. Tiat and Phyr were with us, too—"

He was cut off before he could continue.

Chtholly stood still.

Willem stopped, too, two paces ahead of her, and turned the upper half of his body back to look at her.

"You know that's not it."

Her cool voice criticized him.

"When I said a *dangerous way*, I wasn't talking about us. We were in no danger at all. You were ready to fight the second you sat down on the crate."

Oops.

"No, I wasn't. I was totally relaxed."

"Three seconds."

...

"What was?"

"First you would take down the sheep behind you on the right. After the pebble feint, you would stick the sole of your shoe into his chest, then in the recoil leap, move a half step before the two deer to the right, then lob off their heads to take them out. Those two had knives, so you would pick one up, throw it, and take out two more. That would all be a little less than one second. To render them all powerless like that would be three seconds. Right?"

(Man, I can't believe this...)

She'd seen through most of it.

She was watching his gaze more carefully than he thought. No doubt she was watching everything, down to the subtlest changes in his posture. It had crossed his mind that she was being oddly quiet, but he couldn't believe she had been thinking about this.

"You're overthinking things. There's no way I could fight so recklessly, taking out five guys in one second or ten guys in three seconds like you."

"Don't say you can't. I'm probably the one person in the world right now who knows best how strong you are. Did you forget already? You're the one who taught me how I fight now."

"...Right. You're way too adept a student. I forgot."

Though she said *taught*, it had only been for a few days. And most of that time was spent drilling into her head how to use the Carillon properly.

Even the physical techniques were not much more than paired move sets. He showed her all the named special moves themselves but never taught her the actual names.

Would anyone have predicted that her powers of observation would grow so quickly after just that?

"I'm sure the reason you mentioned for luring those guys out was partially true, but I think it was partially a lie. You could have found a safer way to do it. I don't know why, but—" Her sharp gaze pierced him. "You wanted to fight, didn't you?"

Ah, yeah. He finally realized that possibility when she mentioned it.

Maybe, unconsciously, he wanted to fight. Maybe he wanted to get violent. Maybe he wanted to take the risk pushing his wounded body.

Maybe he wanted to thrust his feelings of distress from sending the faerie soldiers into battle while he stayed behind in safety onto a place that didn't matter, onto people who had nothing to do with him.

"I don't know what you're up to. But stop. You don't have to fight anymore. I... We shoulder your battles now."

"—I have nothing to say to that. You really are watching me closely."

"Because I'm in love."

She spoke calmly.

"C'mon, you're slow!"

Way ahead of them, Tiat waved her hands around angrily. He waved back lightly, and the two picked up the pace.

3. The Road Home, Still So Far Away

"Phew! Finally on our way back!"

As they neared the aire-port, Ithea cried out for joy.

"I'm gonna sleep forever when we get back. I'll be snoring like a man!"

No one bothered to gently remind her of her gender. They all stood side by side, walking silently.

Even without putting it into words now, they were all tired. It went without saying for Chtholly and the others, who hadn't had a proper rest after two weeks straight of fighting, but Tiat, too, after leaving the island for the first time and running about—and being adjusted as a soldier—was just as exhausted.

(*…I have so much to do when we get back.*)

Activating venenum put a strain on the body's blood flow. Blood circulation could go awry or stagnate after using it to fight a long battle, which could worsen the body's condition.

Tired muscles would get better after a bit of rest, but venenum poisoning was different. It could get better after a normal daily routine, but conversely, it could also easily become a chronic condition if repeated over and over in a short time period.

(*It doesn't look like it's clotting enough in weird places to cause fevers, but should I make them take a massage, just in case?*)

He looked down at his palm and lightly cracked his fingers. Though he had lost many of the things he held dear in the past, some of the techniques he'd mastered were, luckily, still useful in this world. Dealing with venenum poisoning was one of them. It was one of his specialties that his former companions (especially the older ones) generally appreciated.

…Well, it wasn't very popular among the younger girls.

If he said it was related to their life span—or, to put it unpleasantly, "service life as a weapon," then they probably wouldn't run away. Probably.

"I wanted to look around a little more…" Tiat glanced back reluctantly.

"You'll have the chance to visit again soon."

When he put his hand on her head, she swatted it away. "I told you not to treat me like a child!" As he pulled his hand back with a bitter smile—

"Second Enchantments Officer Willem Kmetsch?"

A voice without a single hint of affability called his name. When he turned around, there stood an unfamiliar man.

His body was thin and wiry. He wore black sunglasses. His facial features were surprisingly like that of an emnetwiht for a semifer, except for his long white hair and his long, thin ears of the same color.

A rabbitfolk. It was a semifer race, but unlike lycanthropes, their numbers were few. Willem knew that they existed, but it was his first time seeing one in real life.

"…Who are you?"

Willem narrowed his eyes, studying the rabbitfolk's clothes.

He wore a crisp officer's uniform for the Guard. The badge of rank on his shoulder was that of a first officer. The design of his branch of services emblem that showed where he belonged was a shield and scythe—the military police.

·"It is as you can see. I am a first officer with the military police."

The airship was already beginning preparations to set sail. A crew member made his six hands into a megaphone and shouted in a shrill voice, "Please hurry aboard!" If they didn't hurry, then they wouldn't make it in time, and there were no more ships until tomorrow.

"I learned of you through First Armored Forces Officer Limeskin."

"Okay. I don't know what he wrote, but I don't think I've done anything to get the military police's attention."

At least, nothing that big lizard knows, he added to himself.

"Certainly. The first officer wrote, 'possibly interested in young girls' in his report, but that itself does not warrant a reprimand. Personal tastes and interests are not enough to deserve that."

Okay, next time I see that big lizard, I'll start off with a Nightingale Sweep and give him a good, swift kick.

"And even if you did have some sort of predilection that involved the items under your management, it is none of our concern as long as it does not cause any malfunction on the battlefield."

All right, I'm going to pummel this bunny to shut him up right now.

"All lies. It's exactly because he doesn't have any of those interests that I have to work so hard."

Wait, Chtholly, don't insult me like that out loud! It hurts my feelings.

"Then what do you want? You'll need to reschedule if this'll be long, because as you can see, we're in a hurry."

"There is someone who needs to meet with you. Come with me."

"No," he refused flatly. "How many times do I have to say it? I'm in a hurry. You probably know, since you read the report or whatever, right? I'm their director. Taking these guys back to the barracks...I mean, the warehouse, is one of my duties. I don't know how important a first officer is, but I'm not gonna let you get in my way with a simple *Oh, I see, sir.*"

"I cannot have you refuse. I am not here to run useless errands."

"Okay, looks like we're parallel lines here. So how about we make like parallel lines and never cross, and part here?"

As he responded lightly, he tried to slip past the officer. Then—

"The Great Sage, Suowong Kandel."

The man murmured a name.

Willem stopped in place.

"According to the first officer's report, you can adjust dug weapons. And of all things, you hold the position of second enchantments officer. What has been lost has been brought back. In this world, where we have lost the magnificent earth and all the people cling to small pebbles to survive, what that means is immense. Unbelievably so. That is why we cannot leave you alone. You must borrow the Great Sage's wisdom regarding yourself and that technology. Should you resist, then I regret that I would have no choice but to mobilize the military police—"

The man waved his hand lightly.

Accompanied by the quiet shuffle of footsteps, a number of guardsmen appeared from the distance. Though their hands were nowhere near the hilts of their swords, it was unlikely that the long, curved blades slung onto their waists were meant for ceremonial purposes.

"Now, this ain't very diplomatic..."

"Stop, Ithea. Don't use your magic. This isn't like the situation from earlier. If you make a fuss here, we'll be the only ones at a disadvantage. These guys are the type of people who've already considered all that."

"...Understood." Ithea gave a slight sigh of frustration and calmed her magic. "But then what are we going to do? We won't be able to get home like this."

"I know."

As he answered, a single name ruminated in Willem's mind.

The Great Sage, Suowong Kandel.

He knew that name.

One name he could never forget.

"I guess I do have to go see him," he uttered.

"Willem?"

Nephren peered up into his eyes, wondering what was wrong with him. It was unusual for her steel mask to let slip such an easy-to-read expression, but she was just that unsettled.

"First Officer."

"Yes."

"If I go with you, then will your guys take these kids back to Island No. 68?"

All the faeries stirred restlessly.

"On my badge, I will accept your request."

The rabbitfolk nodded.

"Hold on."

A tug on his sleeve.

"What do you mean, you'll go with him? When will you be back?"

"Well… About that, I can only really say once business is finished."

He shrugged. A tinge of anger swirled in Chtholly's eyes.

"Don't go."

"Well, I can't do that, either."

"I'll be mad if you do."

"That's pretty selfish."

"Shut up. You have treated me like a child this entire time, so you should at least humor this much selfishness. Or will you only treat me like an adult when it's convenient for you?"

She had hit him where it hurt.

He was used to dealing with children, but he'd always had trouble dealing with girls who *weren't* children.

He didn't know what she was thinking.

He didn't know what he should believe.

He didn't know what to say to make her happy.

And more importantly—he didn't know what to do to make her stop crying.

"Don't cry."

He reached out with his finger to wipe at her eyes. But his hand was violently smacked away.

"I hate how you're only nice now, of all times."

She was right. He thought so, too.

But he didn't know what else to do.

He was always like this. Especially now. And he would probably always be this way.

"Sorry."

He spoke selfishly and pulled his arm back.

Chtholly's fingers let go of Willem's sleeve, grasped at the air, and with nothing to hold on to, simply balled into a fist.

"...Stupid."

Chtholly muttered, hugging her hand to her chest.

He couldn't stay facing this girl alone any more than this. Willem lifted his head.

"It gets cold on the ship at night, so wrap yourselves in a blanket from head to toe and get to sleep early. If you become cold, then it'll be harder to smooth out your agitated venenum."

"Uh...huh, very well," Ithea responded flatly.

"..." Nephren gave no answer.

"Um, ah, hmm." Tiat busily looked back and forth between Chtholly and Willem, flustered, and it didn't seem like she heard him.

"Bye."

He pushed Chtholly away gently.

He hadn't been very forceful, but she took several unsteady steps forward. After somehow managing to fix her posture, her shoulders shivered.

"Idiot!"

That was all she said, and then she ran off without looking back.

She practically threw her ticket at the crew member and dashed into the commuter loop airship. The crew member, caught off guard by her force, turned around and shouted a belated warning in her direction. "No running on the ramp, please!"

"I've got nothing to say to that..."

Her harsh words seeped into his bones.

"Come on, you guys need to go, too."

"Well, we'll go if you say so, Officer."

As Ithea tilted her head with a dissatisfied look on her face, a cart with sacks piled dangerously high rushed by her. "Whoops! Look out there, little lady," the driver cautioned, which was a little too after the fact, but this was an aire-port, after all. A place where people and cargo were constantly coming and going, and they couldn't stay standing and chatting, even if they were at the edge of traffic.

"Are you okay with this?"

—*Ah, Nephren. Now it's your turn.*

"Okay with what?"

"You haven't said what you need to yet. I will be mad, too, if you feign too much ignorance."

That was new coming from her.

Nephren mad at him? No, he didn't want that.

There was no weirdness in her voice. It was the same as always, or at worst, smoother than usual. That was why he somehow understood that she was being serious.

"I don't wanna make promises I can't keep anymore."

"You don't feel like keeping them?"

"I do feel like keeping them. But in this world, there are things I can and can't do."

"It was you yourself who made Chtholly give such a promise."

He had nothing to say to that, either.

You have to come back. That's what he had said. He forced her to return safely, which would never have been allowed for a disposable warrior, even ignoring her own wishes, for the only unreasonable reason that he just wasn't convinced.

"You don't have the right to say what you can and can't do."

"Okay, okay. I get it. I can't win."

He made a show of violently tossing about his own hair and peeled his gaze away from the faeries.

To be honest, he didn't know what kind of face he was making. He couldn't even grasp the basics, if he was smiling or crying or scowling in anger.

That was why he didn't want to show anyone his cryptic expression.

"I'll finish my work here then head straight back," he announced over his shoulder. "So go on home."

"Mm, understood."

He was sure Nephren was nodding in a place he couldn't see.

"...I'm not really happy with this, but oh well. Out of respect for the promise, we will back off for today. C'mon, pip-squeak, let's go."

"Oh, uh, okay... But..."

"No buts. Let's go."

"Uhhhkay! J-just let me go!"

As Ithea and Tiat clamored, the three faeries' petite footsteps rushed off into the distance. There was the sound of a loud steam whistle that made something deep in his chest clench together tightly. There came a warning from the commuter airship crew member meant for rude customers. "Please refrain from running up the ramp!"

"We could have prepared a ship for them," the rabbitfolk muttered, watching them off.

"They probably don't want you to look out for them."

"I suppose they don't like us very much... Come on now, some of you get going. Escort them to Island No. 68."

Three secret policemen obeyed his orders and ran after the faeries into the ship. The crewman yelled.

The ramp lifted.

The propellers made a piercing sound.

The stabilizing arms released.

Then the airship finally departed from Island No. 11.

Along with the four faeries on board.

—Leaving Willem, his back to them, behind.

"At any rate, you have a very unique way of crying."

The rabbitfolk rudely went to take a peek at his face, and Willem threw a somewhat serious punch at him.

The Immutable Past,
the Vanishing Future
-no news was good news-

1. Soul Chaser—A

Let's turn back the clock a little.

Five days ago.

Island No. 15, before the crash.

✝

A cry that surpassed all reason, that could rip apart an iron sphere with force alone.

In the face of its 178th death, Timere's husk collapsed firmly to the ground. Of course, a crack appeared on its back barely a moment later as its 179th life began to hatch.

It changed form every time it was reborn, and it looked like it chose the form of a plant this time. Visible within the husk of body number 178 was a writhing green mass from which countless vines were emerging as it twisted.

"Cssserulean warrior, pull back! The artillery troopss ssshall begin ssaturation fire to cover your retreat!"

Limeskin's orders flew across the battlefield. But the cerulean warrior, Chtholly Nota Seniorious, was not happy with that. The Carillon Seniorious that she held in her hand was completely in tune with the Beast before her. This Carillon, whose power increased in response to the enemy it resonated with, could essentially display its greatest power of destruction right at this very moment.

In that case, she needed to shoulder this battle for as long as possible.

"Let me kill it just one more time!"

"No!"

A sharp reproach.

For a split second, she hesitated, wondering if she should disobey him and stay.

Overwhelming power was at her fingertips. She was contributing much more than she ever had on the battlefield before. After correctly drawing out the dug weapon's—no, the Carillon's—power, she displayed the true abilities of the Braves, something that had been lost with the emnetwiht.

They couldn't win without her or Seniorious. Surely, they wouldn't mind if she just pushed a little more—

Red Water.

—Huh?

Gray Wind. The Laughing Titan. A Scarred Brow.

—What is…this?

She reeled.

There was no sign or logical connection. All of a sudden, strange images appeared in her mind's eye.

She thought she was distracted.

It had been more than 120 hours since the battle began, after all. It would not be odd for her concentration to slip while she was unaware. And it was a matter of course that her sense of reality would lapse after spending such a long time in a place that felt so surreal. She thought that maybe she was doing something as clever as dreaming with her eyes open.

She had to concentrate.

She could not lose this battle. And she could not die here.

To go home. To return to him. That was why—

Fish that swim in the night. A tower of sand that pierces the heavens. A sun that crumbles into sea green. The sweet throes of death. An armful of cubes.

A red grimoire, locked. A fox's neck overflowing with tall trees. A silver nail. Bakers who work together to paint the entire rainbow yellow and delete every ambiguous color. A headless clown at the bottom of a shipwreck caught in a midnight storm, who laughs and laughs and laughs and laughs and laughs and laughs and laughs and laughs and laughs and laughs and laughs and laughs and laughs and laughs and laughs—

"—Wha—?"

Even when she did concentrate.

Even when she wanted to.

She couldn't keep it at bay.

They kept growing.

Something.

Chaotic images. Disjointed delusions. Self-asserting daydreams. Shadows of the past she shouldn't have been able to recall. Stains on her soul she should have wiped away. The murmurings of someone who stood back to back against her. A reality outside of dreams. Overwhelming turmoil that pushed relentlessly toward her.

"Okay, that's enough."

A familiar voice pierced through her jumbled thoughts.

"Ith...Ithea?"

"I made the suggestion we switch. Here's where you obey and pull back."

"But just a little—"

"If your encroachment advances even a little more, it'll probably be too late."

Encroachment.

A word she'd heard before. Where was it? Oh, right, they told her about it when she became a faerie soldier. What were they, exactly—what were faeries? How fleeting were their lives? What other ways could they die, besides injury?

Faeries were the souls of those who died young and were unable to leave this world.

Their existence could not properly be called alive. It was merely a natural phenomenon, born as a result of the confusion of ignorant souls. That was why, one day, she would fully remember what she was.

"Is that...what this is...?"

"I thought it wasn't going to happen for a while, considering your age. But statistics aren't really reliable, are they? It could be that Seniorious's venenum has forced it along, suddenly exacerbating the condition."

"My age...? A-ah!"

Ithea gripped the back of Chtholly's collar and forced her to withdraw from the battlefield.

The bombardment began behind her. The stalwart lizardfolk soldiers, covered head to toe in armor, stood in a row, lighting their cannons. There was a skull-shattering roar, followed by the shaking of the ground beneath them. The cannonballs, shot without any venenum, mowed down the trees and shaved off the ground, shattering Timere's rebirthing body into a thousand pieces. It of course would not result in a fatal wound—they had to use dug-weapon or Carillon-class enchantments to take its life—but it was useful enough to temporarily halt its regeneration.

Chtholly dangled in Ithea's grip, her golden wings spread above them, flying them to the recess tent 1,200 marmer away from the battlefield.

"Hup."

She practically tossed her onto the floor.

"...Owww."

"Hold on to that while you can. You see a mirror there?"

Still lying on her stomach, Chtholly lifted her head. On the floor, right beside the mountain of crates filled with rations, was a small hand mirror.

"What about it?"

"You'll see."

After listening to what Ithea said to her, Chtholly reached out to it. She grasped the handle, pulled it closer, and peered into it.

Someone with crimson eyes stared back.

"...What is this?"

Chtholly Nota Seniorious's eyes were a deep azure. She wasn't too fond of the color, but Willem once complimented them, saying they were like the color of the ocean, and her opinion of them had changed a little recently. The problem was that she didn't know what the ocean was and whether or not she should take those words as a compliment. But that was a different issue.

No matter how much she stared at them, no matter how many times she blinked, the eyes of the girl in the mirror were a flaming red.

"Those are the initial symptoms. They should subside after two hours of rest, but you absolutely can't use any venenum until then. And think about yourself as much as you can. You can't let someone else's memories take you over. Cling to your own memories."

—*Loneliness in a white darkness. Echoing prayers in a small place. A room full of books.*

Unidentifiable images swirled and raged in her mind as they had been. She tried covering her eyes with her hands and shaking her head, but they didn't disappear so easily.

"These…are…memories? Memories of the person who died when they were little, before I became myself?"

"Someone else. Someone who has nothing to do with you, Chtholly. A complete stranger, with no point of contact with you. The second you forget or misunderstand that, it'll swallow you whole."

"You said something about my age earlier, so is this…?"

"Yup. There aren't many faeries who live very long in the first place, and apparently encroachment from a previous life is such a rare case anyway that most of the time, it can just be ignored. The trends we know from these very few cases apparently show that faeries, fully matured in body and mind, will slowly start to remember as they near twenty years.

"Right now, you're an irregular in an already rare case. Like I said before, it looks like your condition has progressed so far because you kept in contact with a force of venenum beyond your stature for a long time. At the rate you were going, you would've died before the day was over, never mind the end of the battle."

"I don't want that…"

Chtholly rolled over onto her back.

"It'll go away after two hours of rest?"

"Only your current symptoms. You won't be able to push yourself in a fight after this, either, you know."

"…Sheesh."

She covered her eyes with her arm, laughing emptily.

It had been her fate to die in this battle. She was supposed to deliberately push her venenum into overdrive and, by inducing a massive explosion, burn the enemy to a crisp.

But because she didn't—couldn't—accept that ending, she learned from him how to use a Carillon. She learned how to fight as a Brave.

And yet—

How could it be that now, of all times, a death she had never imagined was looming over her?

"It's okay. On the other hand, as long as you don't push yourself, it shouldn't advance too much. Even if it did worsen a little now, you still have a child's body. If you keep to a moderate lifestyle, then you shouldn't have any more incidents of encroachment. It's not gonna cause you any problems in your daily life. I know a precedent for this pretty well, so I'm fairly confident."

She tapped her slim chest.

"…Butter cake, I guess."

"Hmm?"

"I'm thinking about why I can't die, along with an important promise of mine. It's important to cling to my own memories, right?"

"True, but what a selfish memory, eh?"

"Needs deeply rooted in instinct are strong—or probably something like that."

"Sure." Ithea laughed.

Chtholly felt like it was the first time she saw her smile in a long time.

When she thought calmly about it, that didn't sound right. Ithea was always cheerful in a not very refined way, always smiling and grinning and beaming and smirking, to the point that it was hard to remember any other expression but that.

"Well, I'm off."

"…To where?"

"The front line. Ren's next, and she should be hard at work right about now, so I'm her support. We'll buy a lot of time for you, so stay calm and keep still."

"Okay… Thanks."

"As you say."

Ithea's eyes narrowed into slits, and she nodded with a smile.

She had a question.

Why was Ithea this knowledgeable about past-life encroachment?

How did Ithea see through Chtholly's changes so accurately?

But she couldn't ask.

There was no reason to.

"Here we go!"

Ithea activated her venenum, spread her wings, and flew into the sky.

She saw a shimmer of crimson in those golden eyes.

†

Quarreling adults. A big, big puddle. Chicken feet.

"What weird memories."

A murmur.

A warped lake. An endless orange-colored road. Shimmering silver fabric.

"Souls that died when they were babies become faeries, huh? It really seems like they recognize a lot for babies. Where in the world was this child born?"

Or maybe…

Maybe she just didn't know, since she was "born" as a faerie who was already somewhat aged, and that was how the world looked in the eyes of young children.

Take a small lizard dashing through the forest. To them, it might be a dragon spewing flames, or it might be a guide beckoning them to another world, or it might be the handle of someone's bag that had come off and was rolling around in the wind in their eyes.

That was why the world that spread before a child's eyes—to the eyes of someone not a child themselves—was filled with mysteries and absurdities. Maybe that was what she was seeing now.

"…Tsch."

She lay on her back, gazing at the inside of the tent. So her tears rolled down her temples and toward her ears.

They say faeries come into existence when young souls who cannot fully understand death go astray.

And as far as she knew, there were no faeries who lived long enough to be called adults.

She'd always thought it was because of the fighting. Starting from the oldest faeries, they'd each get hurt in the intense fights with the Beasts, or they went into overdrive and scattered to the wind.

Or could it be that she was wrong?

Could it be that, in the first place, faeries were beings who could never become adults?

The shadows of the souls that never comprehend death grow up and, in the end, understand death. Then everything comes undone, and they return to nature.

This was probably what fate would feel like if it existed.

No matter how hard she wished, how hard she prayed, she could not overturn what had been decided at the beginning.

"I was planning on pushing him, though, *'If I live long enough to be an adult, then you have no reason to complain, so marry me.'*"

She'd heard it from Willem. Once, in the emnetwiht world, one of the qualities necessary in a Brave was *tragedy*.

Those who shouldered pasts and destinies that anyone would grieve over were much more suited to be Braves, individuals who wielded tremendous power, than those who didn't. That's apparently how it was.

And Seniorious, the oldest and mightiest of Carillon, especially favored those with such tendencies. Only those burdened with fates of death and destruction could wield the virtuous white blade.

"—I get it... That's why you're letting me, of all people, use you."

She glared at Seniorious, which lay on the floor.

Faeries were intrinsically flippant about their lives, perhaps because they were made from souls of the dead. They didn't really fear death.

In that sense, Chtholly was now in a situation that was not very faerielike. She had a reason she couldn't die. She had a place she had to go home to alive.

"Butter cake."

She balled her hand into a fist and murmured those words.

—All right, all right. Okay. I'll make you eat so much cake, you'll get heartburn.

—You understand, yeah? So you have to come back.

What came to mind was the promise she made with him that brilliant, starry night.

Her determination solidified.

She didn't care anymore if she would never be allowed to live long.

She didn't care if she never matured into an adult by his side.

She hated to admit it, but she would give up on that. It was her fault for being born as a faerie, of all things. That just meant she was unlucky enough to be liked by some tragedy-loving Carillon.

But. *Because* of that, at the very least.

She wanted to live just a little longer in this ephemeral dream.

Even if the world would end one day, it would still continue to exist until the moment it ended. That was where she lived. So—

"Okay, let's go!"

She mustered up a show of bravado and raised her fist into the air.

✝

And the fight continued.

The sun set, rose, set again, rose again. Over and over.

✝

There was despair.

Despair took the form of a giant faceless being, made of black ivy that twisted around itself.

That was the Hidden Beast Number Six born from Timere's 216th death, its husk in the face of its 217th death, the pupa birthing from its 218th life—

—and the cradle for something else birthing from it.

"Another Timere…?"

The lizardfolk soldier murmured, forgetting about his bombardment.

"No," Nephren, exhausted to the point of collapse, denied under her ragged breath. "The tactical sensors didn't say multiple Timere would attack. The sensors are absolute when it comes to Timere's attacks. This is something else."

"But the artillery isss not working! Isss that not Timere?!"

"By process of elimination, it is a Beast besides Timere that no one knows…?"

"Why'd this thing have to pop up *now*?!" Ithea cried, half in tears and half in laughter.

Everyone was exhausted due to the long battle. They kept on killing Timere, telling themselves that this would be the last time, that this would be the finishing blow. In the end, this was the situation they arrived at.

The cannonballs and the gunpowder for the cannons the lizardfolk were using had almost emptied out, as had their physical energy.

And a never-ending battle otherwise was draining their morale. The fact that the number of enemies had actually increased, not even to mention whether or not they could kill them, was enough for everyone there to pray for their spirits.

They couldn't win.

Everyone was thinking it, yet no one could put it into words.

"—We sshall retreat."

It was Limeskin who announced that, his voice hard.

"In twenty minutess, we sshall lift the ressstraintss covering thiss island. At the ssame time, sssend a warning to all neighboring islandss. We have failed in our removal of the alien enemy on Island No. 15, and the island sshall hencsseforth become a threat to all life asss we cssede territory to the Beasstss."

"Wait, wait, wait, wait!! That's really, *really* bad! Regule Aire is still floating because none of the Beasts can fly at will! We can just start the countdown to annihilation if we let them build a nest so close!!"

"That iss exactly right. That iss why we musst sssink thiss island asss quickly asss posssssible. However, thiss island isss big. If we hope to drop the island, then our ussual firepower is not enough. We musst focusss off all Regule Aire's collective firepower. It will be a racsse against the Beassstsss' ssspeed."

"...Let me just ask to make sure, but what will happen if we lose the race?"

"Do you really want to know?"

"Uhh, nah, I'm good. Thanks."

She covered her ears and shook her head.

"—It's my fault," Chtholly muttered, her face recognizably pale from even a mile away. "Had I gone into meltdown alone like I was supposed to, then it would have easily gone down. Only because I said I wanted to live, this—"

"No," Nephren interjected, crouching firmly on the ground, beyond her line of exhaustion. "The tactical sensors can only calculate Timere's enemy's strength. Even if you did self-destruct, Chtholly, it would only just barely defeat Timere. That other Beast would have stayed behind. Then we would have ended up fighting this unknown Beast without you. That is a situation infinitely worse than this one now."

"Man… So rational… This predicament is bad enough as is, but, well, it's just a bit better than the worst of worst-case scenarios, so you could say you saved us a bit."

Ithea's mouth twitched.

"You…think so?"

Chtholly wore an expression of disbelief.

"Yes," Nephren declared strongly. "They were not enemies we could win against to begin with. Once we decide to consider that so, then we should now think about how we will sink the island."

"That, too, iss logical." Limeskin nodded. "Ssshould we gather all the artillery under the Winged Guard'ss dissspossal, then no matter how much we hurry, it would likely take ten nightsss. But if there isss no damage to other islandss in the meantime, then we may begin to ssee the ssseedss of victory."

"…It sounds like we'd be walking on really thin ice by then, but how certain are you that all that firepower could sink the island?"

"About twenty percssent."

"Wa-ha-ha, that's way too realistic; I can't laugh at that."

"Absssolutely."

The lizardfolk general laughed, a sound like a pebble rattling round in his throat.

Oh, right, Chtholly thought.

It was surprising how easily her heart accepted that this world might end.

Nothing felt unusual about that statement. She felt no need to reject it. It felt like something that had shadowed her for her entire life had suddenly come to rest on her shoulders, in her hands.

This world was ending from the beginning. Now it was simply reaching that point.

The end, which had been continually put off, was finally here. That was all.

There was no need to mourn. Everyone would die. Nothing would be left behind. Not a single person would feel sad or lonely. So the best option would be to face the time with mind at ease when it came. Panic and fury would bring nothing good.

(—But I can't let that happen!)

She unconsciously gripped the brooch at her breast.

She hadn't forgotten. She had a reason she had to return home alive. She could not die until she stuffed herself full of victory butter cake. She had to live until that blockhead accepted her proposal, even if that meant subsisting off mud. Yep, it looked like she had no choice but to live a long life.

And to do that, she couldn't let the world destroy her.

Of course, Willem couldn't die on her, either, and she didn't want to think about exposing the little ones, who couldn't fight yet, to danger. So—

A rocking boat.

—Ugh, that encroachment again.

She let her mind slip for a fraction of a moment, and it came bubbling out from the gaps in her consciousness. It was after her own life. How annoying.

She, as an unstable being who was a faerie, might have been in the weaker position, but what did she care? She was alive. She was alive and in the pursuit of happiness. She would never let some person who'd died ages ago take that right away from her.

The moment she decided that, a thought came to mind.

That was not the smart way to do it by any means. If she thought more carefully about it, she could probably think of much better ways. But now, right at this moment, she was limited in thinking time, and she felt like the plan she came up with was already the best plan.

What she needed to put her plan into action was just a bit of resolve.

—Resssignation and ressolve are, in esssencsse, the sssame thing.

—Both indicate the abandonment of sssomething important for the ssake of one'sss goalss.

Right. She would resign, proudly and with confidence. She would abandon what was important to her for her goal. That was what she needed now.

Slowly, she took in a deep breath.

And slowly, she took the time to exhale.

"Chtholly?" Ren called to her, probably thinking she was acting strange. She did not respond.

"I thought of something. First Officer, begin the retreat immediately," Chtholly quietly advised, staring straight at the squirming Beast. "Ren, Ithea. Help me out. You can fly on your own, and you can get to the airship even if your escape is delayed, right?"

"What are you talking about?"

"I'm going to break this island."

She announced, swinging Seniorious in her right hand.

The countless cracks in the blade widened. The faint light indicating the agitation of magic poured from those gaps.

The Carillon were made for weaklings to stand up against overwhelmingly powerful opponents. That was made possible by the mechanism that used the power of whatever came in contact with the blade. The stronger the opponent, the more powerful the Carillon became to confront it.

And now, before them, was a terribly mighty opponent that could destroy the entire world that was Regule Aire.

"Well, then."

There were only a few seconds left until Timere's 218th life would finish birthing.

Chtholly kicked off from the ground. The awakened venenum in her body heightened her concentration and stretched out the flow of time. She pushed aside the walls of air that surrounded her in this gray world, now devoid of color, and closed the distance in a single breath.

The vines coiled, ready to attack.

Chtholly deliberately studied the tangle of eighty-seven vines.

Though there were many of them, most of them were bluffs meant as a threat. Sixty-five of them would uselessly smash to the ground if she left them alone, and she would not need to worry about evading them. The problem was the remaining twenty-two. Eight were aiming at her legs to take away her mobility, five were aiming at her arms and Carillon to reduce her offensive ability, and the remaining nine were aiming for her head and chest to end her life. Looking carefully at each one showed they weren't moving particularly accurately, but since there were so many of them, it would be impossible to avoid them all. If this was a suicide attack, then she would just have to endure the fatal wounds and think about moving forward, but she couldn't rely on such easy-to-read methods. So—

(First!)

She cut away at the vines aiming for her legs and, at the same time, had Seniorious learn the magic flowing inside the vines that touched the blade. The light pouring from the cracks grew stronger.

Chtholly's thoughts and physical speed quickened. The increase in speed bought her a little more time. Pushing into that gap in time, she brandished her sword. The five vines aiming for her arms scattered into the air in pieces.

(Next!)

The seven-eyed frog.

The encroachment quickened, too. She couldn't be bothered about it now, so she ignored it.

The magic within Seniorious grew even more excited from the five freshly cut vines.

*   *   *

The lion that swallowed the snake. A mountain of coins.

The same thing happened again. She concentrated on mowing them down with her blade, as though she was satisfied as long as she could make contact, starting with the ones closest to her. The power she gained every time she did so was enough to give her time for her next flash and next step.

A mountain rising from the sky. A hazy, rain-drenched rural town. Candy in a small bowl.

The distance between them became zero.

She stabbed the Carillon into the entangled mass of vines before her from above.

The sword sliced through several of the vines, penetrated the mass itself, and pierced straight into the earth of Island No. 15.

A burning guidepost. A round rainbow. Castanets playing haphazard noises. A cat of gold-and-silver-streaked fur. A wheel rolling upward. A double-edged knife without a grip. Gloves as large as mountains. A man hanging from a tower—

(*—How do—*)

Seniorious bellowed in response to Chtholly's will. The venenum, brimming with overpowering heat, ignored her enemy Beast, releasing all its power into the tip of the blade that stuck into the ground.

"—you like—"

The blade of the Carillon itself dazzled brightly.

Starting from the hilt, the shine gathered its way toward the tip.

"—thiiiiiiiis?!"

All the light vanished into the earth.

There was a short breath of silence.

Fwoom.

There was a low, dull sound that reverberated in her stomach. Cracks appeared in the ground.

They spread out like a spider's web, enveloping the entire island. Light poured from the cracks. The light widened the cracks from within the ground. The ground split.

The island sank.

The Beast spread its vines wide, haphazardly clinging to the bedrock around it. But the rock it clung to itself was collapsing, so it would not help support it no matter how much it struggled.

As though being buried in the heap of collapsing rubble, the Beast faced the surface and began its fall.

"_____"

Chtholly thought she heard the Beasts yelling something as they fell.

But of course, she knew it was nothing but her imagination.

"Are—are you out of your miiiiiiind?!"

Ithea flew with her illusory wings, raising her voice in a cry. In the end, she picked Chtholly up, who lay almost clinging to the Beast as she was all out of power.

Nephren, who'd followed her, beat back a hit from the vines that attacked them from behind.

"I can't believe how reckless…"

They flew to an altitude that was just out of the vines' reach. Before them, Island No. 15 was beginning to fall.

Though the island had only a 20 percent chance of falling after gathering the entirety of the Winged Guard's arsenal, it easily collapsed from the power of a single Carillon.

"Chtholly, can you hear me?" Ithea asked, carrying the cerulean faerie.

"Mm… I'm fine; I can hear you…"

"Do you know what you just did?"

"I'm fine… I remember…"

"You're not fine! Do you remember what kind of situation you're in? Didn't I say that pushing yourself will only advance your encroachment quicker?! Something like this means way more than just shortening your life a little bit, you know?!"

"I said... I'm fine; I'm fine..."

Chtholly lifted her head and smiled.

She narrowed her bright crimson eyes and grinned weakly.

"I promised I would go home. Right?"

A fleeting smile, on the verge of vanishing.

"I'll go home proudly and tell Willem. That because of him, I'm still alive. But we don't know what tomorrow will bring, so please teach me all you can while I'm by your side."

There was spirit in her laugh.

"...Oh, but I guess I have to keep the encroachment a secret, huh? I'm sure if he heard about it, he'd get really worried. I want him to stay how he always is: a little lazy but sort of cool and dependable."

"Oh, geez, you're not very attractive with your feelings leaking everywhere!"

Ithea embraced her precious friend's thin frame as hard as she could.

"That hurts, Ithea."

"It's proof you're alive. Deal with it."

"Oh well," Chtholly murmured and relaxed.

She promised she would return home.

She could live because of how she clung to that promise.

That was fine. The problem was what came after. Once she fulfilled her promise, once the promise was no more, what would become of her life?

Ithea asked nothing of this natural question. Chtholly gave no answer.

Because she did not want to know the answer.

Because until the day she could no longer run from it, she didn't want to look.

2. The Protectors of the Azure Sky

There also happened to be an old man here.

Few knew his name, but on the other hand, he himself was very famous. The people referred to him as a distinguished wise man—the Great Sage.

His history was that of Regule Aire.

Let's say one turned the Grand Senato Library, prided as one of the greatest collections on the island cluster, inside out and found the oldest history book it had to offer. Since it was from a time without papermaking and printing technology like today, it would probably be of thick parchment and handwritten in pen. Flipping through the pages would show the record of the founding of Regule Aire. A time when the surface began to face its destruction, wrought by the Seventeen Beasts released by the emnetwiht. A time when the few remaining survivors had gathered on the summit of The Holy Peaks of Fistirus, unable to do anything in the face of rapidly advancing death. That was when a single man created a road into the sky with powerful venenum and led those still alive onto land in the heavens.

That single man was, in other words, this old man here.

Even the history books, whose duty was to speak of the past, could not tell of an era older than the wrinkles on the old man's face.

That was how long he had lived with the land and led the people.

"A man who can adjust dug weapons?"

His sharp, wide stare cut across the corridor. The female prima officer, who brought the news, went pale and shivered in fright.

"Oh—no, I'm not reprimanding you. I was born with this expression in my eyes; no need to be afraid. Never mind that. Was the one who brought this absurd story Baroni Makish again?"

The officer nodded vigorously.

"I swear, that man. Can he not see the simple difference between truth and lies? It is impossible to adjust dug weapons. That would be like the sun rising in the west, or midsummer snow, or the emnetwiht brought back to the land."

The officer's head tilted, as though she had a question.

"What?"

He turned his gaze to her, and she gave a little yelp and shrank again.

"—I'm not reprimanding you. If you have doubts, then ask."

"U-um! It is nothing but captious wordplay! Please, forgive me!"

"Captious… Ahh, were an emnetwiht to be revived, he could adjust emnetwiht weapons, you mean."

The officer responded, "Yes," in a faint voice.

"I am telling you not to be so afraid. There is nothing wrong with wordplay; a heart that enjoys fun is precious, especially for those who live a long time. And that doubt is reasonable. Even I, were I in a position where I did not know anything, might think the same. However, it's wrong." The old man shook his head. "Dug weapons, or Carillon, are made up of count-less talismans and linked together with enchantments—it sounds simple enough when put into words. Discovering new powers through the mutual interference of differing talismans, much less the word *refined* itself, was a miracle established on a lukewarm balance. Of course, the technology needed for that adjustment was beyond proper course. Would you under-stand if I likened it to stacking natural stones that were not quarried one on top of the other to reach the heavens?"

"Uh…"

She stared blankly at him.

"Even among the Braves, who carried these into battle, there were barely even a handful who could look after their own swords. That was normal. If someone wanted to repair their Carillon, then they had no choice but to gather a team of specialist engineers and spend time doing so at a fully equipped workshop.

"And despite all that, what was this report? He adjusted it by itself? *And* it was the strongest blade, Seniorious? And the same man even adjusted the other swords? Ha-ha!"

He spat it out, almost enjoying it.

"It is probably an exaggeration to sell himself, but this is too much. Such a monster that managed such skill did not exist even in the emnetwiht world. This isn't the rebirth of a miracle; it's just some big talk way beyond that."

"A monster…? I recall you using those words before. It was the Black Agate Swordmaster…yes?"

"Ah—right."

The old man's mood improved slightly as the officer led to the next topic.

This corridor was needlessly long, and there wasn't much to look at. He wouldn't be able to stand all the walking without even the most meager of small talk.

"That man may have been able to make that big talk into reality." The Great Sage spoke of him, his eyes gazing into the distance in nostalgia. "It was terrifying how much of a mystery he was. He didn't really have any talents that could be called a talent. The venenum he could produce was below average. He could not even produce simple thaumaturgy. Even on the path of swordsmanship that he chose, he could use nothing greater than the moves he learned at his public training hall."

"Was he…a normal person, perhaps?"

"Quite. The most normal of normal. At the very least, that is what he should have been in the beginning.

"However, he wished to become a Legal Brave. And no matter how many times he was presented with the reality that he was talentless, he never gave up on that path. He did all he could to take on as many things as possible in order to bury what he lacked. And he did all he could to cultivate the few things that he made his own. In the end, what happened? Born was a monster, who, in a battle outside the emnetwiht realm that was crawling with beings who held legendary swords and could unleash legendary techniques, brought and fought techniques that were no greater than what one could find at the average training hall, achieved the greatest military results, and came home safely."

It was dread, or respect, or perhaps something else. The Great Sage's body shivered slightly.

"Even I, who was still immature at the time, was a few steps ahead of him in regards to the power I could wield and the breadth of the things I could accomplish with that power. And yet, even now, after I have gained even more power, I cannot imagine being victorious over him if we fought."

"Imagine?" The officer hung her head and smiled conservatively. "We do not know what sort of things these legendary swords and techniques might have been. To say that he was more of a man of valor than you are, Great Sage, then I cannot even begin to imagine as such."

"——Perhaps that is a good thing. Things that are lost will never return. Memories of that time, recollections of those from that era, are all nothing but my nostalgia. You, who live now, should live carrying this era on your shoulders." With an audible step, they stopped walking. "This room?"

"Yes. Are you ready?"

"Well, I've been brought all this way, so I have no choice. At least let me look upon the face of the swindler—"

The knob turned, and the door opened.

A young man with black hair sat with his knee resting on the reception desk, yawning in boredom.

"...Hmm?"

The young man looked at him.

"Hey, Suowong. Nice to see you—man, you really changed your look, huh?"

The Great Sage's jaw dropped to the floor.

"You got real tall, didn't you? I almost didn't recognize you, since you're not wearing your cape."

"The Black Agate...Swordmaster...?"

With a hoarse voice, the Great Sage—Suowong—called the young man's name.

"Been a long time since I've been called that, Magus of the Polar Star. Glad to see we're both doing well."

†

Suowong Kandel.

Like Willem, he was a member of the band of Braves assembled more than five hundred years ago to defeat the Visitor Elq Hrqstn.

Suowong was the favored disciple in the Imperial Tower of Sages, a thaumaturgist who hid in himself rare abilities. His power, which could crack the ground and pierce the heavens, was on the level of Quasi Braves wielding Carillons on the battlefield. Though he had fatal flaws in his naming and fashion sense, and though he was a little shorter than other boys his age, and though he was a little too confident in his own abilities, he more or less lived up to his legendary reputation. He most certainly had enough talent that he took pride in himself and enough diligence that he did not let that get to his head, which allowed him to work hard, and he had enough humility to recognize the skills of the people around him, and he had enough cooperativeness to unify these people and powers for the sake of one goal—he had it all.

To Willem, he was a companion whom he could rely on without a doubt—and one he could confide in. Of course, that was not something he could tell the man himself.

And naturally, he thought Willem died fighting five hundred years ago.

However, since that wasn't the case—and since he had been acting as a prominent authority figure since the birth of Regule Aire, there were some things that fell into place.

It had always struck him as odd. Many things in this island cluster were based on the emnetwiht and their culture.

It was not natural in the first place that a great many races escaping to the sky after the surface was destroyed led directly to their building towns and thriving. Normally speaking, suddenly gathering all these races, which had lived separately on the surface, would have immediately sparked sectarian conflicts, leaving only the strongest at the top of society.

Additionally, it was also strange how all the architecture bore a striking resemblance to the things that emnetwiht once built.

Back on the surface, the semifer lived in the treetops and in the cracks between stones. Orcs piled up dirt and made their dwellings in things that looked like trenches. Lizardfolk lived in tentlike houses, made of braided grass. Ballmen and prima and similar races had no concept of housing.

These kinds of people were all gathered in one place, everyone on their best behavior, building towns that were a striking copy of emnetwiht settlements, and beginning to live there—that was not something that happened naturally.

There were countless other things Willem could point out. Food culture, the coin system, garment manufacturing techniques, social systems, paper manufacturing and bookbinding systems, and so on and so forth. The skies where everyone but emnetwiht lived bore an unbelievable resemblance to the world the emnetwiht did live in; it was almost impossible to find exceptions.

Now, he could easily point to a solution in regards to all this unnaturalness.

It was Suowong's doing.

In the creation of Regule Aire, he was the one who had come up with the plan of the skyward civilization itself by demonstrating intense leadership.

He was from the Empire, and he was knowledgeable in history. And the Empire's history was a repetition of invasion and annexation, so it was a treasure trove of precedent and an example of those born in different cultures gathered together in one place. That was why he didn't find it odd that Suowong pulled off creating and leading a singular world culture.

After all, he was a universally acknowledged genius.

✝

"You were petrified on the surface?!"

The stern-faced old man raised his voice in hysteria.

"No matter how hard we searched with the heart-rate detector back then, we found no responses, so we were certain you'd died—"

"Well, I was petrified, so my heart wasn't moving. That heart-rate detector of yours tracks inherent venenum before it's activated, right? You would've never found me."

"—Give back the tears I cried that day."

"Huh? You cried for me?"

"N-n-no! I'd never do anything like that for you. I knew you were like a cockroach; *ooh*, I knew it!"

He floundered about in frustration, and it didn't suit him at all.

"You say that, but it's been pretty rough on my end. I never heard people could be revived after being turned into stone until that happened to me. Back then, I didn't think any help would come, so I assumed I was dead. The doctor's bill was pretty high just for treating everything besides the petrification. It took a lot of time and money to release the multiple curses and spells that bound me. So thanks to that, I've been living life in debt since the moment I woke up."

"This is ridiculous…"

Willem thought he heard Suowong grumble, "That's why I don't like you," as the old man gazed at the ceiling.

It wasn't like he turned to stone because he wanted to, and he wasn't revived because he wanted to be. He had things he sort of wanted to say back, but he understood how he felt, so he kept silent.

"Forget about me—what about you? I heard the emnetwiht all died out? Well, even if they didn't, it's been a long time since then. Looks like you've aged a lot, but how are you still alive? Don't tell me there are others still running about, too?"

"Don't ask so much all at once. You're too excitable. Well, one answer can explain those three questions," Suowong said, removing his coat and exposing his chest.

There was a large cavity in the place where his heart should have been.

"That's…"

"I was killed in the battle five hundred years ago, too. I was fighting Jade Nail. One of three Poteau guarding the Visitors. It was Emissa and I who fought against it, and the two of us were easily killed. But before I lost consciousness, I improvised and cast some thaumaturgy on myself. I can't explain to you the detailed theory behind it, but it interfered with how my life works and fundamentally changed it so that I cannot die via conventional means. So now, I will not die of wounds or old age. And of course, now I'm—not an emnetwiht anymore."

"Oh…"

"Let me just say this beforehand, but don't pity me. I am rather fond of myself now, and to have you sympathize with me sends shivers down my spine."

"No, not you. I'm more shocked to hear Emissa was killed."

"Hey!"

But you seem on top of it no matter how I look at you, he thought but decided not to say.

"That explosive devil is gone, huh? I thought I had enough of being sad, but man, does it hurt to hear it again. So I guess the others died in the battle, too, huh?"

"No—not everyone. Lillia and Navrutri lived."

Suowong hadn't survived beyond time like Willem, who had turned into stone. He had lived for five hundred years until now, his eyes open, moving around. So he should know everything that happened while Willem slept as a dumb rock.

"Hey—"

He had a mountain of things he wanted to know. He was about to ask.

Where did the master go while we couldn't get ahold of him?

What happened to the army of monsters marching on the capital?

Did the princess and king, who had always supported us, survive?

"Just tell me one thing. What are the Seventeen Beasts? What happened, and where, to draw those things out while we were off fighting the Visitors?"

He swallowed most of what he wanted to know and asked just one thing.

The outcome of Lillia's fight. The safety of his companions. There was no point in checking on that now. His race had died out a long time ago, and he already knew the answer.

What he should at least know now were things that were worth knowing.

"—Do you remember the True World?"

He nodded. It was one of the armed cults that revolted against the Empire's governance at the time, five hundred years ago. At the request of the royal family, Willem and the others under Brave Lillia crushed them.

"The remnants of their organization…apparently set up a base in a small town outside of the Empire and began research on biological weapons or such. Those Beasts were the results of their research."

"I see. That's why they say the emnetwiht destroyed the world."

Though the people directly responsible were just an extremely small portion of the emnetwiht, it was all the same to the other races, who were on the verge of extinction. And no one wanted to bring back the honor of a race that died out long ago.

"…According to the military police report, you're now working as an enchantments officer, correct?"

It wasn't a topic he really wanted to talk about, but Suowong had clearly changed the subject. There were still things about the past he wanted to know, but he decided not to go against him.

"Just on paper, so I feel bad for the real enchantments officer."

"What are you talking about? You think there's a second enchantments officer besides the one on paper?"

"Huh?"

Suowong looked irritated when he saw Willem staring at him blankly.

"The second officer has different qualities than those of the first or third and below. That is to say, it's a fictional position for internal and external appearances, to show that enchantment research, which we all know is not making any progress, is being conducted anyway. The only thing in the job requirements is to *exist*, and nothing else is expected. Because the real work is research that is already being conducted under the presupposition that it will never make any headway. Even progress reports would be a waste of time and paper.

"I will say, however, that it isn't as though there is no precedent for a warm body to fill the position of second officer. But that's when we politically demote a troublesome officer. They receive nothing more than the minimal power and pay, and it is rather useful as a final useless post... In the end, it's a job that isn't much more than what's on paper." There, he sighed deeply. "What represented our discontinued research was investigating the laws of the Carillon. So you being the second officer might shake up the very reason the second officer exists."

"That's fine; no one's gonna worry about it. I'm glad I can relax at a useless post. I'm not gonna ask for any more power or pay than I already have."

"—Aaaargh!!"

Suowong put his elbows on the desk and grasped his head.

"What's wrong?"

"I don't know if I should call you the right man for the job or if I should liken you to a battle-ax splitting walnuts. You're the only one who can pull off the feat of maintaining the Carillon, and that would be the best choice militarily, but to keep you there for the rest of your life would be such a disservice to all of Regule Aire..."

He was muttering about something, but the second half he spoke in such a quiet voice, he couldn't hear.

"Oh yeah, that military police officer said I should ask the Great Sage about what I should do with my treatment. Sorry to ask while you're distressed, but can you decide quickly, please? I promised 'em I'd go home right away."

"Go home?" Suowong lifted his head. "Go home to that faerie warehouse?"

"I have no other home, do I? I don't think my house on the surface is still around. Sure, since it's our first time meeting after a long while, I guess we could renew our old friendship or whatever. We both are fortunately doing pretty well. Let's just reschedule for another day."

"No... Wait—" He faltered. "...Before that, there's someone I want you to meet."

"What, again? It's been two days since I got here. There are kids at home who'll go hungry if I don't get back soon."

"He'll want to meet you once he knows you're alive. And you— Well, you probably never wanted to see him again. But you can't ignore him. You can't."

That was a strange way of putting it.

"What? Someone I know? And since you're a mutual—an old acquaintance?"

Suowong didn't respond.

"Don't be so pompous. Who is it? I'm a regular emnetwiht; I don't know a single other person besides you who could've lived for hundreds of years—"

His words stopped in their tracks.

Someone he met in the old world. Someone both he and Suowong knew. A timeless, undying being.

He realized he could think of one such entity.

"—No way."

"We'll finish our talk while we walk."

Suowong spoke bluntly, getting to his feet.

"Wait, I didn't say I'd go yet."

"Then will you say you won't go?"

His words caught in his throat.

Suowong must have taken that response as his answer. He flung open the door, faced the officer who stood waiting there quietly, and announced with a loud voice:

"We are going to Island No. 2. Prepare the airship immediately! …Oh, no, no need to be afraid. It's not your fault. It is mine for raising my voice. I should have opened the door calmly. You don't need to shrink down so much, really."

✝

Island No. 2.

Also known as "The Pith of the World Tree."

Looking at Regule Aire from directly above, it was almost right in the center.

So of course, it sounded like it would be an important place of trade. However, not a single one of the presently active airship routes came to this island.

There were three reasons.

One was that there were no settlements of any race on this island, so there was no value in traveling to it for trade. Another reason was that it was not only floating much higher than the other islands, it was also constantly surrounded by storm clouds, so regular ships could not even get close.

And the final reason was that it served as a sanctuary.

Fundamentally, all things fall down. Despite that immutable rule, more than a hundred islands were floating in the sky. This mysterious secret that was the premise of this world called Regule Aire lay within this Island No. 2. And so it was taboo to brazenly enter and violate its hallowed ground, as it might send Regule Aire plummeting straight to the earth.

And yet, sometimes, failed salvagers announced, "I'll expose the truth covered by this so-called faith!" and they went up carelessly. Most of them got thrown off course by the thick clouds enveloping the island, sudden turbulence, and storm clouds, and without ever catching a glimpse of their goal, they ended up returning in tatters to the island they came from.

There were times when salvagers claiming to have seen beyond the clouds appeared. According to the stories they told while battered and covered in injuries, the island wasn't a naturally floating rock like the other islands but a lump of polished black crystal, and there were countless plants growing naturally on it but the seasons were all off, with both spring and autumn flowers blooming everywhere at the same time, like a chaotic daydream. Of course, there were very few people who believed such idle gossip, and the mystery that was Island No. 2 continued to fly high in the azure sky, shrouded by the veil of the unknown.

"…That's a huge black crystal—no, wait, a flowerpot?"

"Yes." Suowong nodded casually. "To be more precise, it's apparently something like a giant talisman, but I don't know exactly how it works. I don't feel the need to analyze something that big, either."

"Look, the inside of the pot is full of all sorts of trees."

"Yes. The island is apparently covered with a small weather-control barrier, completing the seasons inside only. The storm clouds around it are a by-product of it. I'm not exactly sure why it does that. I did hear that it's a sympathetic model meant to control a larger barrier, though."

"You don't know very much, do you, Great Sage?"

That remark must have gotten to Suowong, as the wrinkles between his brows deepened.

"A sage is what someone who knows what they are supposed to know is called. Someone who knows nothing says he must know everything."

"Whoa, that was a bug, a bug! This place is full of things that don't know what season it is!"

"Listen to me when I talk to you!"

Island No. 2 was rather small for an island. There didn't seem to be any place that could be an aire-port. He wondered how they would dock without a place to lock in the anchor arms, but the small airship the Great Sage had prepared easily landed on a flat, open plane.

"Wow, this is great. Let me have one. It looks useful for shopping."

There was quite a distance between the faerie warehouse and the aire-port. That made it a little inconvenient to go shopping on other islands.

"Don't be absurd. It is priceless."

"That's too bad."

They stepped onto the island.

It wasn't a big island; however, it was much bigger standing on it in person. He took a look around, and the unsettling view of plants from all different seasons jumbled together filled his vision.

"The hell is this? Apples and peaches growing together?"

"Go ahead and have one if you're hungry. They're not poisoned."

"Nah, I don't think so…"

The thought that they might be using some sort of questionable fertilizer crossed his mind. He would hesitate to touch it, much less put it in his mouth.

"And? Is that where we're going?"

In the center of the island stood something that looked like a black crystal tower, probably made from the same material as the island's base. As far as he could tell now, it looked like it was the only building there.

"It's black, covered in thorns, feels just like an evil temple, so it must be it."

"Correct… I've known him for a long time, but I still don't understand his taste."

"I'm not so sure if you're saying that." He chuckled. "Did you ever get cured of your love for that white cape after five hundred years?"

"Don't say it like it's a disease. This is policy and my very soul itself; I will not be tossing it away even after a thousand years," he huffed.

He could feel the tears welling in the backs of his eyes at how nostalgic their conversation felt. He was with a companion he thought he'd never see again, having a sort of chat he thought he'd never have again. That was enough to make him feel so comfortable right in this moment.

"Hey."

"What?"

"Thanks."

"…Why must you thank me now? I do not understand."

"Just felt like it. Don't worry about it."

Suowong was the Great Sage, but that didn't necessarily mean that the Great Sage was Suowong. He had been on his own for five hundred years. He'd gained new things during that time, and he himself must have changed. The way he referred to himself and his manner of speaking couldn't stay the same as it had been when he was a boy.

That being said, Suowong now was acting and speaking just like the Suowong from long ago. Why? Probably because Willem was with him.

Losing one's companions, loved ones, home, and everything else—Suowong had already experienced this pain once in the past. And he knew that now Willem was in the same situation. So he was deliberately acting the way he used to in the past, in order to help his retrospection, even just a little bit. That was probably it.

"Why are you grinning? It's making me uncomfortable."

…And it wasn't entirely impossible that he was just reliving his own childish innocence. He didn't want to think that after he'd voiced his thanks.

The tower was empty.

They pushed open the heavy double doors, headed up the spiral staircase that exuded such an air, and entered something that looked just like a throne room, but it was completely empty.

"What is the meaning of this?"

"It is not unusual. The weather is nice today, so he must be out for a walk."

"Wha…?"

"Look, as you can see, there is nothing else on this island besides plants. There is almost nothing to do in one's free time, so he wanders about outside on nice days." Suowong neared the window as he spoke. "See, just as I thought." He motioned downward with his eyes.

He could see a lone girl wearing a maid's outfit pushing a cart.

"…What about her?"

As he thought absently of how it wasn't a deserted island, he observed the girl. The angle was too sharp, so he couldn't see her face, but upon seeing the triangular ears popping out of the top of her head, he could tell she was a semifer…probably an ailuranthrope. Considering how she kept her form despite how heavy the cart looked, he thought she must be proficient enough in cargo transport.

"Not her. Over there."

He directed his gaze the way Suowong was wagging his finger, and there, riding on the cart the girl was pushing, was an armful's worth of a black something.

It must be a weight stone, he thought. But something wasn't right. It was hard to say what that was right away, but it was the texture, or the mass, or something like it—

"Hey, you piece of trash! We let ourselves in!" Suowong called down with a thunderous voice.

"*—Oh, it's you, Great Sage! Perfect timing—I was just enjoying a bit of free time!*"

The black thing moved.

It was a skull. That was the shape it was in, at the very least.

It was pitch-black, big enough to fit comfortably in the arms of an adult. It looked up at them and moved without anyone touching it and even spoke in a deep, elderly male voice, but even if he ignored all the other things, it was, without a doubt, a skull.

So, yep.

At the very least, it was not just any skull.

"*We couldn't finish our game last time. This time, we shall put a clear divide between black and white!*"

What gave Willem a headache was how he recognized that voice.

Only two years ago—just to Willem, though, for time had passed hundreds of times longer than that—he had, without a doubt, met the owner of that voice. And that moment was carved into Willem as an intense memory, one he would never be able to forget.

"My apologies, but I did not come today to make merry or soothe your boredom! I have someone I want you to see, Ebon Candle!"

Between the top and bottom of the tower, the two elderly men exchanged threatening—yet familiar—words in loud voices.

"What… We have a guest?! You fool, you mention that first!"

"I was going to, but you are the one out of your seat! Keep a communication crystal nearby if you're going to complain! Then I can leave a message before visiting you!"

"What nonsense! You know communications don't work around the barrier!"

"Then you should do something about a problem like that! An immortal pillar of a god should be able to figure out at least that much!"

"Well, your mouth has certainly gotten bigger after just five hundred years of life, hasn't it! Wait there—I'll give you a beating on the board!"

"I already told you that's not why I've come today!"

"Oh, right! Kaya, my apologies, but quickly!"

Ebon Candle called her name, and the maid girl nodded slightly, setting off into a run as she pushed the cart. It made a loud rattling noise as they came around to the front of the black crystal tower and ran up the spiral staircase.

"—By the way, Suowong." Willem groaned, pressing his fingers hard on his temples. "I'm having a bad dream right now, right?"

"I understand how you feel, but face reality. If you want, I can hit you."

Suowong brought his tightly balled fist before Willem's eyes.

"No, thanks. If you punched me now, I think my head would explode before I woke up."

"Well, that's disappointing."

The turbulent rattling was quickly nearing the throne room.

"Ha, ha-ha-ha-ha-ha-ha!"

It felt like a strong gust of wind came from the throne.

The pressure of venenum was so overwhelming he could feel it on his skin without any Sight. Willem knew of only one being that could produce such a thing. Only one.

"What a long time it has been, Brave of the people! To think the time has come round for us to meet again after so many years; it truly is a coincidence!"

It was one of the three pillars, a Poteau. They protected the Visitor Elq Hrqstn, enemy of the emnetwiht race, and stood before the group of Braves who tried to attack it, making them the strongest and final barriers.

"But how unfortunate, in the end, we are beings destined to battle each other! This reunion gave us a miracle, but alas, it cannot escape the path paved with blood!"

This being had many names.

Such as, "The One Who Dozes in Death."

"The Weaver of Worlds."

"The Father of the Great Earth."

"The One Who Burns the Flame of Darkness in the Garden of Light"—Ebon Candle.

It was an old enemy that none other than Quasi Brave Willem Kmetsch defeated in exchange for his own life in battle long ago. However, just as he mentioned on the verge of his own death, he was now reborn in this world after a long slumber—

"—Nah, I think I'll pass on that."

Willem's expression twisted in annoyance, and he waved a hand.

"Hmm, I see. How unfortunate."

The skull—Ebon Candle—quickly and easily withdrew its venenum. The overwhelming presence that filled the throne room withered and vanished in an instant.

"I assumed you had pent-up hatred for me, so I played the role to play on that."

"How you show your consideration is fatally ridiculous, you know."

"Hmm? Are you saying you feel no hate?"

"Even if I did, you think I'd bother with a rematch? The last time I fought, I had things I wanted to protect behind me, and you were the thing that was going to destroy it. Now's different. So I have no need to fight. Right?"

"To keep no grudges while fighting to the point of throwing your life away... You are a more openhearted man than I thought."

"Well, I wasn't planning on that. But even if I did have a reason to fight, what's up with you? The Ebon Candle I fought before actually had flesh and bone and a body below the neck. So why are you only a head sunbathing in a cart?!"

"What do you mean? It was you who burned my body!"

"Yeah, I know that! But you said you'd wake up after sleeping for a hundred years! You'd usually think that means you would get restored completely! Why's there barely even half of you?!"

"Like I said, it was your fault. You destroyed me so thoroughly that my body wasn't quick enough to regenerate in a hundred years. Do you understand my shock when I woke up? Though I don't have any tear ducts, as you can see, I wanted to cry!"

"Like I care!"

"Since then, however, I've continually been in a state where I must use my power, so I haven't had the chance to recuperate. And so, as you can see, after four hundred long years, I am living in disgrace."

As it spoke, the black skull tilted deftly on the throne.

While he was uncertain if it was "living" in disgrace with a form like that, it didn't matter right now.

"—Okay, enough. Suowong. You didn't bring me here just to say hello, did you? Hurry up and get to the point."

"The point?"

"All right." With two pairs of eyes on him, Suowong nodded. "This is a terrible man, whose personality, character, temperament, disposition are all rotten, down to his core, but his skills are top-class and reliable. He would be a talent who would be sufficient—no, indispensable for implementing our plan."

"Hmm..."

"Hey, c'mon, Suowong, what are you talking so casually about?"

"Don't you want to take back the surface, Willem?"

"I know when you change the subject like that you're— The surface?"

There was a word Willem could not overlook.

"The surface is devastated, and isn't it a danger zone where the Beasts run amok? What are you talking about?"

"We will attack... But of course, the surface is much too big to take it back all at once. First, we attack and conquer the closest point to Regule Aire, the summit of The Holy Peaks of Fistirus, and make it the base of our counterattack. What we need is a way to fight against the Beasts. And a way to continue the fight. Until recently, we've lacked the latter. But now that you are here, we are much closer to solving that problem. The Carillon, now in bad condition and unstable, will once again thrust into the battlefield. This is a huge step forward."

"Huh," Willem responded absently, nodding slightly. "That's a grand plan."

"Isn't it? Of course, it's a very long-term plan and will require all the cities of Regule Aire to come together and fight. There are big risks, and we may not get results right away. However, the final chance of victory is big enough." As Suowong spoke, his speech became more and more worked up in excitement. "We can *create as many faeries as we want*, so our only problem has been the number of Carillon."

"———Huh?"

Again, he responded absently, nodding slightly.

The color in Suowong's face changed when he noticed his loss of words.

"No, wait, that was—"

"No need to patch things up, Suowong. I had a vague idea. Ebon Candle used necromancy in our battle together. The feat of coming back to life after a hundred years has to be an extension of that. And the thaumaturgic spell you cast on yourself as you were holding on has to be in the same category as necromancy. And you two are protecting Regule Aire. Right, I've got the gist of it."

According to Willem's research, faeries were lost souls of young children who didn't understand their own death. They were originally unstable and ambiguous beings, natural phenomena that took the form of will-o'-the-wisps and gnomes. And apparently, there was a technique in necromancy that could create them artificially and put them to work.

Furthermore, the leprechauns Willem knew weren't will-o'-the-wisps or gnomes.

They might be unstable. They might be ambiguous. But they most certainly had hearts like those of emnetwiht girls. Without a doubt, they experienced hope, fear, love, dreams, attachment, and despair in those hearts of theirs. And on top of that, the girls fought with their lives on the line to protect Regule Aire.

"Anyone could figure it out with all this information."

Indeed. And he could make a guess with firm conviction.

Willem, driven forth by a strange feeling he could not grasp that trapped him between tears and laughter, put into words the conclusion he came to.

"You're the ones producing leprechauns, aren't you?"

3. The Flow of Time Since Then

He'd heard that the end of the hallway on the second floor was leaking recently.

When he went to go see for himself, he saw how it might require a little handiwork. Since they'd have to call in someone from town later for proper repairs, all he had to do now was some emergency fixing up. He needed some wooden boards and—

"—Hey, you know where the hammer is?"

Willem turned around.

(It's in the closet downstairs. You used it before! Did you forget already?)

Chtholly put her hands on her hips and responded in annoyance.

(Honestly, I don't know if you're just forgetful or if your memory's bad...)

Her lips pouted, but her complaints made it sound like she was having a bit of fun. But before she could finish complaining, she noticed something off.

Willem wasn't looking at her.

(What are you looking at?)

She turned around. But there was the hallway, as always. No one was there. Nothing was there.

"Where's Chtholly?"

That was an odd question.

Willem voiced the strangest thing as he looked around.

(What kind of joke is this? I'm right here.)

She complained in a stronger tone than she had before, but Willem just said, "Weird, I thought she was right here," tilting his head, and didn't look to her at all.

(Come on, I'm right—)

She wanted to reach out.

She couldn't.

The hand she reached out with was nowhere to be seen.

When she looked down at her body, she realized it was not there.

"Chtholly? Where're you hiding?"

Willem walked off.

He wandered all over the faerie warehouse, searching for the girl he could no longer see. He couldn't find her. He left the warehouse and made rounds on the island. He couldn't find her. He called over anyone he could find to the side of the road and asked the whereabouts of Chtholly Nota Seniorious. No answers.

(Hey, where are you going?)

(Where are you searching?)

(I'm here.)

(I'm right by your side.)
(Hey.)
(Hey!)
(Listen!)

No matter how hard she tried to talk to him, she had no voice. Her voiceless words reached no one.

Willem finally tired of walking and stood still, puzzled.

Someone placed a hand on his shoulder.

"You need to accept it already."

Nygglatho said gently, a sad smile on her face.

"Those girls are dead."

—With a start, she threw back the covers and sat up straight.

Her heart wouldn't stop pounding. She covered her thudding chest with her hand and took deep breaths. Just when she calmed a little, she shivered. The cool winter morning air relentlessly stole away her body heat through her pajamas.

She got down from her bed, scooped up the blanket, balled it up, and hugged it tightly.

"A dream?"

Chtholly was murmuring to herself.

"That was…a dream."

She lifted her head and looked to the window.

Dawn broke later in the winter. The world beyond the curtains was still enveloped in darkness.

Her body felt heavy. She wanted to roll herself up in the covers and lie down again.

But she didn't feel like it.

She couldn't close her eyes, since she might see what came next in that dream.

✝

It had been two whole days.

Two whole days since the battle on Island No. 15 ended.

Since Chtholly and the others came back to the faerie warehouse.

Willem still hadn't come home.

✝

The rain that poured raging billows at dawn abruptly stopped like a dream just before noon.

With the energy of bounding jewelweed, the little girls raced onto the field under the bright azure sky. A white ball flew high in the sky and, before long, became covered in mud. The girls who chased happily after it, too, were quickly covered in mud.

In the corner of the reading room, Nephren slept.

She used her arms, folded on top of the table, as a pillow, her expression calm, her breaths quiet.

"Aw, geez, it's not every day that Ren throws books on the ground," Ithea said as though comforting a child as she picked up a book from beneath the table. "For her, it looks like she's just physically worn out, rather than being fatigued due to overuse of her magic. It's not been that long since she matured, so her strength hasn't caught up yet." She stroked the hairs on Nephren's forehead, murmuring praise of how well she'd fought in such a long battle.

"...By the way, are you doing okay, Ithea?"

"Me? I'm so okay my nose could bleed. Right now, the only thing I'm confident in is living a long and lazy life." She chuckled and puffed out her slim chest.

Chtholly wasn't so sure.

This golden faerie always, always said important things in a way that made it hard to tell if she was serious or joking. And so when anything important came out of that mouth, she was never sure if she should believe it or not.

"And how about you, Chtholly?" she asked in return, her tone nonchalant.

"Me? I'm, well…"

Totally fine, of course, is how she almost responded.

She wanted to say it.

She couldn't. Behind her lightweight words, Ithea's gaze was so sharp it pierced straight into Chtholly's eyes.

"…I guess things are a bit tough. I feel like I'll be turning down missions for a little while." She shrugged, smiling weakly.

"If it's really bad, then, I know we were just there, but you could petition them to let you go back to Island No. 11? You are crucial firepower right now anyway, so they'll probably accept, and if you let the doctor know what's up, he might give you some advice to ease your mind?"

"I'm fine. It's just a little tough." She waved her hand. "I'm happy enough to just get advice from you. I trust you, *miss*."

"…I'm happy to hear that, I guess."

"And can you imagine how awful it would be if I left, and he and I switched places? I want to see him as soon as possible, so waiting at home after he tells me to go back first was the right answer."

"*Sigh*… You really are a girl in love."

"So what?"

"You're not hiding it or lying about it anymore?"

"Well, he'd avoid it even if he knew how I felt. I'd never get ahold of him if I hid it while approaching him boldly. So I don't think I have a choice now but to stay open and break through head-on. He looks aloof, but he's actually surprisingly delicate if you break his pace, you know."

"Yeah, true."

"And so when he gets home, I plan to keep pushing and pushing him. I'm of course going to be asking for your help then, so are you ready?"

"Okay, leave 'im to me!"

Ithea gave her a thumbs-up. Chtholly gave one back.

There was nothing false in her words.

Once he got home, she was going to push and push him.

Indeed. If he came home.

He hadn't always been around.

So the way things were now without him was how the faerie warehouse was originally meant to be.

"He might not come home."

The moment she grew just slightly discouraged, those kinds of thoughts crossed her mind.

"I mean, he doesn't look very bright, but he's such a rare talent. Rather, the fact that he stayed in a place like this all this time was weird. He's supposed to be someone who all of Regule Aire would go to see, put in a suitable position, and beg for lost wisdom and stuff like that. So the right choice for him is probably to never come back."

When she said that in front of everyone, there came various responses.

Tiat and the other little ones made a ruckus: "We'll never allow that!" "I don't wanna be sad." "I'm the one who'll defeat the officer!" "What's a wisdom?" It was hard to tell if they understood what she meant or not.

Nygglatho reasoned with her: "You should perhaps be a little more honest." *Shut up, I know that already.*

Nephren just lowered her gaze slightly and showed no other reaction. Well, it was very much like her.

And Ithea responded with her own question through a mischievous grin: "If that's true, then what are you gonna do?"

If he never came home, then what would she do?

She thought about it, but she couldn't come up with any particular answer.

"Nothing, probably."

She responded with a vague expression, and Ithea sighed a deep, deliberate sigh.

*   *   *

He was never here in the first place.

So the life she was living apart from him now was the one she was meant to live.

"Yaaaaah!"

There came a sharp yet adorable-sounding battle cry, and her body reflexively slipped out of the way. Missing their mark, Pannibal and Collon came flying from behind her and fell straight onto the hallway floor.

"…What on earth are you doing?"

She helped the two up, her voice annoyed.

"I told you so!" Tiat came running after them and lightly flicked each of their swollen red noses. There were two small yelps of pain.

"You guys are no match for the older kids, not in ten years," Tiat hummed, her chest for some reason puffed out in pride.

"But I can't practice without Willie around, and my techniques will get weaker!" Collon protested, tears welling up in her eyes.

"What techniques are you talking about?"

"Techniques to take over the world!" Pannibal balled her hand into a tight fist.

"What world are you talking about?"

Tiat rolled her eyes, and beside her Lakhesh apologized profusely, pitifully shrinking in on herself.

"…By the way, Tiat?"

"Yes? What is it, miss?"

"Your aptitude for maturity has been checked, right? Did they finish the compatibility confirmation for a dug weapon yet?"

"Oh, not yet. Nygglatho said we'd look for a partner once Willem came back."

"…I see."

She ruffled the little girl's hair.

"M-miss?"

"I hope you get a good sword," she said gently and pulled back her hand.

"What's wrong, miss? You look pale."

"Really? I guess I'm still tired."

Chtholly smiled vaguely and escaped the younger girls' gazes.

✝

When she returned to her room, she immediately closed the door and leaned against it.

And just like that, she slid down until she sat on the floor.

Her head drooped, her arms cradling both that and her knees.

"You liar..."

Chtholly's voice was quiet, so that no one besides herself could hear.

"I kept my promise. So why didn't you...?"

After a while, she lifted her head and stood.

With both the door and the curtains shut, the room was as dark as night. But she knew her way around her own room, so by the faintest of light, Chtholly reached out to the mirror lying facedown on her desk.

"..."

Within the darkness that spread on the other side of the mirror—

—sat a person with red eyes.

A flat spider.

"Who are you?"

Her voice shook as she questioned the one opposite her in the mirror.

What should have been there was a face she knew well. A face she saw every morning when she washed. A face she saw smile, cry, grow angry, and everything else her entire life should have been there.

So, why?

Why was the person in the mirror staring blankly back at her?

Why, when she saw that face, did she think it was a stranger?

If that was the face of someone she didn't know, then whose face was it on this side of the mirror, in the place she could not look at directly?

*　　*　　*

A half-eaten cookie. A candle stub and a burned envelope. A metal bird and a rainbow-colored arrowhead.

Shut up.

Shut up, shut up, shut up.

She couldn't help the memories. They came out on their own.

The battle was long over. She hadn't used any magic since. Was she not okay, then? Was it not supposed to interfere with her daily life, as long as it stayed moderate? Was what Ithea said a lie, then?

No.

It was her fault.

During the battle, she'd tossed away what was important to her in the name of her resolve. She traded almost all the remaining time she could stay herself for the miracle of Island No. 15's collapse.

She had no regrets. No, she couldn't have any. Regule Aire was on the verge of destruction. The life of one faerie soldier, meant to be disposable anyway, had just shortened a little, so it was supposed to be a good bargain.

What she should regret was how she showed off to Willem after that. Because she didn't want him to worry. Because she wanted to go home to the Willem who was simply thinking about their future together before she left. And so she would stay completely silent about her past-life encroachment, even forcing Ithea and Nephren to stay quiet about it, but by the time she realized it, she was already in her current state.

She at least wanted to tell him here, *I'm home.*

And—

"I wanted…butter cake…"

She murmured, the tears in her throat.

The girl in the mirror moved her lips, as though she said the same thing. A single tear rolled down her cheek.

A cracking world. Fish swimming among the stars. Dad. A yellow stuffed animal. A strange girl with cerulean eyes. A twisted tree. A cat that keeps meowing and meowing and meowing. A pebble wrapped in paper. A bright, cloudy sky. The world beyond the mirror. And. And.

The mirror slipped from her hand.

It shattered on the floor, and the pieces scattered.

The girl slumped over on the spot.

4. Once That War Is Over

"You're the ones producing leprechauns, aren't you?"

The two accepted this conjecture without a word of denial.

"We are not producing each and every one individually, actually. We simply performed a rite to the giant soul that acts as the base material so that they would be naturally born with physiques and characteristics similar to those of emnetwiht." Suowong's expression stiffened as he explained with a creaking voice.

"And we also revised the miniascâpe barrier that surrounds Regule Aire so that the souls would not fall to the surface. Now, hearing this explanation, what will you do?"

Meanwhile, Ebon Candle's expression showed no signs of changing (of course, that's assuming a black skull could have different expressions). There were no significant changes in his tone, and rather, it felt like he was carefully observing Willem's response.

Willem wordlessly grabbed Suowong by the chest.

He held up a balled fist with his other hand and aimed for the side of Suowong's face.

They stayed like that for several seconds.

"Beating you up...wouldn't accomplish anything."

Denouncing the faerie system itself would help nothing. The powers of the Carillon were necessary in protecting Regule Aire, and emnetwiht Braves were required to use the Carillon's powers, but since they were nowhere to be found, leprechauns were produced in their place. Disrupting any part of that flow would lead directly to Regule Aire's destruction.

Not only were there no other alternatives, this was the best possible solution.

There was no room there for ethics or humanity.

The girls' battle was not the product of someone's ill will.

Even Willem himself, who claimed he couldn't fight, was on the other side, pushing Chtholly and everyone else onto the battlefield. No matter how unsatisfied he was with that, no matter how much it pissed him off, he couldn't blame either Suowong or Ebon Candle.

"—But that's just to maintain the line of defense. The Braves fight to protect all the towns they and the people hold precious. They're not meant for expeditions for increasing territory. Don't waste them on a fight they don't need to fight." Willem groaned as he let go of Suowong.

"It's not a fight they don't need to fight. They will have to someday. You understand, don't you? Regule Aire isn't eternal. We've somehow managed the past five hundred years, but that does not mean the next hundred are guaranteed. We will one day have to return to the surface."

"It's only you and me who think that, though."

"—What do you mean?"

"There are only so many people who've seen the world as it was five hundred years ago, before what it is now. To those who haven't, the surface has been a faraway land their entire lives. It might be a treasure island of dreams and adventure, but it's nothing more than that. Their precious homeland is the sky they live in now, the islands they live in now, the cities they live in now. There is nowhere else but that."

He looked at Suowong, expecting agreement.

"Yeah, but...aren't you...upset?! Don't you want to go home?! I've lived here for five hundred years! Far longer than I did on the surface! The sky is without a doubt my second home! But still! My first home is the Imperial Capital! You feel the same, right?! No, you should feel so much stronger about this than I do, since you just got here! You can't have forgotten!"

"Even if we did devote all of Regule Aire's power to reclaiming the surface…"

Willem responded ever so quietly in contrast to Suowong's outburst.

"Who is there? Would there be any family there to welcome us home?"

"That's…"

Suowong faltered.

He opened his mouth to say something once, but he quickly closed it.

"Will you not tell him?"

"No."

He shook his head, and his expression tensed.

"So that is your will, Willem Kmetsch."

His voice changed.

Willem's old friend Suowong Kandel was already gone. Standing there in his place was the five-hundred-year-old Great Sage, who shouldered Regule Aire's future. His soft blond hair had faded; his once apple-smooth skin had withered, covered in wrinkles; his doll-like stature had grown into that of a giant; and…

The young genius with a promising future was now risking the present and the future to seize the past.

"Sorry, *Great Sage.*"

He forcefully plastered a strained smile on his face to keep it from twisting in sadness.

"Looks like I'm not cut out for fighting for the world's distant future anymore."

"…I thought you were more of a Brave than that."

"Yeah, me too."

He nodded.

There was a time once when Willem possessed ambition and the title of Quasi Brave, but he eventually reached a stage where he could go no further.

He thought it was the fault of his talent.

He thought it was the fault of his circumstances.

But maybe, just maybe, he was wrong all along. Perhaps somewhere deep inside him hid a more fatal defect.

"I thought so, too. I truly believed I could become a Brave. But I couldn't. That's why I'm here now, living in disgrace."

"Hmm. Let me ask you another question."

The skull's voice came from beside him.

It skillfully rolled from the throne and fell into the cushioned cart. Without a word, the maid waiting by its side pushed the cart, bringing it to Willem.

"This is what you said when I was provoking you earlier: You have no reason to fight. And even if you did, why has the great being that was Ebon Candle, who could pierce the heavens, fallen into such an unassuming form, though being as charming and dignified as he is?"

Willem had no recollection of saying any of that. At least, that last part.

"You so cleverly changed the subject, but it does not seem entirely fair that only I tell you the truth, no? Even if you had a reason to fight, is there any other reason why you cannot?"

"What?"

The Great Sage raised his eyebrows slightly.

"Sure." Willem nodded generously. "I sure don't have it as bad as a skull, I know, but my body has barely recovered from the battle with this guy. The petrification is gone and so are the enchantments, but there are tiny wounds left all over my body, leaving me little more than a worn and tattered rag. A troll I know said to me, 'I wouldn't even have to pull out a knife to pick off your meat; it's so full of tears that I could just rip into it with my teeth alone.'"

"I see. So now, that is to say, you do not have the fighting power as you once did. Even if you did wish to fight, you cannot. So—for example, if we were to forcefully subdue you right now, you would have no way to fight back. Is that correct?"

"Oh, I get it now."

Willem scratched his head.

"Honestly, I wish you wouldn't. I know this sounds cliché, but I've got people waiting for me at home."

"Your life is precious to you, is it?"

"Nah. I just have no way of getting home after beating you to a pulp."

He shrugged.

"I don't know how to fly an airship, do I?"

"...That doesn't seem like sound logic. How nostalgic; you haven't changed a bit since then, have you?" With a somehow delighted tone, the skull rolled to face the Great Sage. *"Great Sage. Give up for now. This man holds steady. Rather...he seems like stubbornness incarnate. He holds only one purpose within him. He sees no value in anything that has nothing to do with that goal. So he will not bend. He will not stop. He will persist.*

"Once he has decided he will protect those faeries, that becomes his entire world. He will protect them, even if it means sacrificing anything and everything else. I do not wish to be struck again by those incorporeal incantations."

Nah, I wouldn't do that.

Incantations weren't that easy to wield. Most of the ones Willem used back then no longer had their activation conditions fulfilled. It wasn't that he didn't have any he couldn't use anymore, but if he did use them, the price he'd pay would be his life or, if he was supremely lucky, then become stone again, which might be his end anyway. Either way, he couldn't go home to the faerie warehouse.

...And he wouldn't bother kindly explaining all that. It sounded like he was being overestimated, and he felt like it would be best to let Ebon Candle keep believing that.

"But—"

"If you wish to say something, then you must tell him everything. The man's attitude may change if you expose one or two secrets of the surface that you've kept hidden."

"That's—!"

The Great Sage raised his voice, his expression flustered.

"...Secrets of the surface?"

On the other hand, Willem furrowed his brow, sinking his teeth into a phrase he couldn't let go.

"What is it? What are you hiding?"

"...It has nothing to do with you."

"You're such a liar. From the way he's talking, sounds like it's important enough to change my mind. And?"

"I shall say nothing."

"Okay. Well, Great Sage?"

"I shall say nothing as well. This is about the future of this world. It's something I can only tell to those who are concerned for the future."

You bastard, this is some first-class revenge for earlier, huh? Now aggravated, Willem was about to argue back, but—

There was the sound of footsteps coming up the spiral staircase.

"Lot of guests today, I see."

Ebon Candle murmured, irritated, and everyone turned their gazes toward the door. What appeared there was—

"Pardon me."

—the rabbitfolk first officer.

"This is a sanctuary. I told you never to come here without good reason!"

The Great Sage reprimanded him, his voice low and thunderous. The rabbitfolk nodded slightly and bowed. "I came prepared to be scolded, but something happened that requires an urgent report."

"—What is it?"

Unlike his previous tone, the Great Sage urged him on in a calm voice.

The rabbitfolk's gaze darted toward Willem for a brief moment before he leaned in to the Sage's ear, relaying some sort of information.

"...And you made the judgment that this required urgent passage into the sanctuary to report?"

"Yes."

He nodded earnestly at the Great Sage's odd question.

"Very well. I shall tell this man myself."

He slowly shook his head and took one step toward Willem.

"...What now? Does this have to do with me?"

"Indeed it does, Second Enchantments Officer Willem Kmetsch," the Great Sage announced with solemnity. "There has been contact from a partner of the Orlandry Merchants Alliance. The user compatible with dug weapon Seniorious has begun to lose personality due to past-life encroachment. While physical dissipation has not yet begun, it is only a matter of time."

✝

The pale-faced Willem left the sanctuary on the officer's ship.

The remaining two watched the sea of clouds he vanished into, a heavy silence over them.

"Why did you not tell him everything?"

Ebon Candle asked, breaking the silence.

"If he knew what was on the surface, what remains on the surface, then his response may have been different."

"Probably."

The Great Sage replied, his face looking as though he had swallowed something bitter.

"But as a result, it would most certainly shatter his spirit. Such a fellow who can keep fighting on a singular conviction can do nothing when his heart is broken. While a rusted halberd can still be used, a destroyed spearhead cannot."

"Success depends on how you convey it. Are you not skilled at controlling people by manipulating information?"

"Sure. He is a simple man, and I could easily control him now, but..." He shrugged lightly. "Go ahead, laugh. It's nothing but personal sentiment. I once secretly looked up to him as an older brother, and it seems I do not wish to lie to him."

"Such consideration is all well and good, as long as it does not go to waste."

Despite the lack of lungs, Ebon Candle gave something that sounded like a sigh.

"A faerie broken once never returns. If that man is unlucky, then he will soon crumble."

5. What Happened to the Promise

He had no recollection of how he managed to get home.

That military police ship should have taken him back to Island No. 68 from Island No. 2. Barring course adjustments for replenishment stops and avoiding dragon stones, they should have taken the shortest route in the shortest time.

And yet, no matter how he hurried, as a matter of course—

—Willem didn't make it.

A girl with cerulean hair lay on the bed.

She looked as if she was sleeping peacefully, as though she would open her eyes and begin moving at any moment.

But she didn't.

The girl would never wake again.

"She kept her promise." Ithea stood in the doorway, informing him in a quiet voice. "She came home alive. She came home with a sliver of life left after leaving a battlefield she should not have survived, thinking only of the hope that she would see you again—lean on you again."

"Ithea." Nephren, standing beside her, shook her head quietly. "Don't blame Willem. We were the ones who didn't tell him about Chtholly."

"True. I'm not planning on blaming him for that. But—"

"...Right. You should blame me for not keeping my promise," Willem murmured. "She did what I asked her to. But I couldn't even greet her properly. That's what this is about."

✝

Death was perpetually a part of daily routine for a faerie soldier.

They were aware of how little value their lives had. And so once they lost a companion of theirs, they were not terribly sad about it. They did not wear their hearts out by doing such things. And so, their capabilities as weapons did not suffer.

"Um, um, guys, do you know where Nygglatho went?"

Lakhesh entered the playroom, looking around every which way.

"No. Do you need her?"

Collon asked in turn, practicing her attacks on the joints of a blue stuffed animal.

"Yeah. I wanted to ask her what to do about shopping on the weekend. It's almost blizzard season, and I think we probably need to do some stocking up."

"Yeah, we can't fight on an empty stomach!"

"...Nygglatho should be in the mountains," Pannibal answered, kicking a white ball against the wall on the carpet. "That's where she always goes when someone doesn't come home. This is probably the same."

"Oh...okay."

Lakhesh understood.

"Are you going to look for her?"

After a moment of thinking, she shook her head. "No. If she's gone, then that means she can't show her face to us, right? If I go all the way to see her, she would probably eat me."

"Likely." Collon nodded gravely.

"A valid judgment." Pannibal agreed honestly.

"...Tiat?" Lakhesh called the name of the last of them, who wasn't participating in the conversation.

"Huh? What? Sorry, I wasn't listening."

Tiat had thrown herself onto the carpet and lay there, staring at the ceiling. She hurriedly sat herself up.

"What's wrong, Tiat? You've been distracted lately."

"Er—" Tiat was aware of that. So when she searched for a response, her words briefly caught. "...I dunno. My head feels empty."

"Because Miss Chtholly's broken?"

When she heard that, something in Tiat's chest stung. But she didn't know exactly why that happened, so she brushed it off as her imagination.

"Maybe. I dunno."

She tilted her head, misjudging Lakhesh's question.

†

Slowly, ever so slowly, time passed.

One day went. Another day. And another day.

Time flowed like a river eroding away stone.

†

No matter how much he concentrated, the magic inside Chtholly was doing nothing but flowing calmly, and he found no abnormalities.

Enduring the headache that came with using Sight, Willem took Chtholly's hand. It was pale, small, cold. He gently massaged several points by her knuckles on her palm.

"—Long ago, there was a guy who lost consciousness from sudden-onset venenum poisoning, and he never woke up. This technique brought him back. It's very non-stimulating, and slowly, confidently, you use it to fix the flow starting from the body's extremities—"

He knew it would do nothing.

Unlike that time long ago when his companion barely made it out with his life, there were no abnormalities in the venenum in Chtholly's body. That meant there was nothing to heal. This wasn't the cause of her disorder.

No matter how many external tricks he tried, not a single one set things on a good course.

But he couldn't do nothing. There might be some sort of tiny effect somewhere. He clung to that hope, so faint he couldn't call it a possibility. He had to do something to keep himself occupied from how he could do nothing.

He never welcomed her home.

He never heard her say she had come back home.

That amassed regret made him cling to the illusion that there was a way for him to make amends now.

"Willem."

He heard a voice from behind him and turned around.

"Hey… Haven't seen you in a while, Nygglatho."

"Yes. I'm sorry—I was away for a bit. My heart breaks whenever someone dies here. I always feel like I'm strange for being sad, yet I don't want to feel that way, and my head just goes in circles. So I went into the wilderness and took it out on some trees and some bears."

He felt bad for the trees and bears.

"How strange this is. Once this happens, I lose my appetite. Even though there's such a soft and delicious-looking piece of meat before me—"

"I don't think you're allowed to be a troll anymore."

"I know. Do you think I could change into something different now?" The troll in her apron dress smiled weakly. "I'm tired of crying, yelling, and being angry on my own." Nygglatho's profile was, just as she said herself, colored with the deep hue of exhaustion. "How terrible this all is. I'm a bit happy right now. That you're crying for her. It makes me feel like I'm not alone."

"That really is terrible, but I feel the same."

When Nygglatho appeared here, he felt a little like he'd been saved. He would admit that.

"—I do have something I need to talk to you about. I want to change rooms, so will you come with me?"

"We can't talk here?"

"I don't think I could. And I think it would be hard for you, too."

Oh, he got it. That was the kind of talk she wanted to have.

"Can I run away?"

"I won't stop you if you did."

Ah, damn it. He couldn't run anymore once she said that.

*   *   *

Nygglatho's room was dark.

Only now did Willem finally notice several things: that it was night somehow. And that it was apparently raining outside.

"I'm sorry—this is the only lamp I have with oil left in it."

She placed a small oil lamp for reading onto the table.

The dim light lit the room with a faint glow.

"Would you like something alcoholic to drink?"

"That's new. You never offer anything but tea in this room."

"I have no fire, so we have no choice. And…"

It would be easier to talk drunk. Words weren't necessary to finish that sentence.

Willem blew the awkward atmosphere away with a single sigh, and he asked, "—What do you want to talk about?"

"Right." Nygglatho paused slightly in hesitation. "It's about the test to see which sword would be compatible for Tiat."

"Oh…" He nodded vaguely. "Seniorious?"

"You know it well."

"It makes a big difference in combat power depending on whether the user is ready to use the sword or not. Thinking normally, once the first person's broken down, it starts looking for the second… I'm not thinking normally… I can't believe I said that without a second thought. I'm gonna barf."

"I'll rub your back if you throw up. Because I empathize with you. But don't forget that you have to think about getting used to this. This isn't the first time this has happened, and it won't be the last."

"And every time it happens, you interrupt the bears while they're busy hibernating?"

"How rude. I at least bring home the parts I've won to turn them into a stew."

She wasn't arguing with him at all, but that sounded important to her.

"Well—I understand the logic behind the combat power and stuff, but

Seniorious is a completely perverted blade. I don't think it'll sync up with the next person just because it's convenient for us."

"What do you mean?"

"It's the oldest of all holy blades. It completely outclasses all the other swords. And its class translates directly to how selfish it is when it chooses a user. Seniorious is very picky about who wields it."

"Can you do something about it with your strength?"

"Of course not. If I could, I'd use it myself." Willem smiled bitterly, recalling an event in the past. "When I first saw Seniorious, my master was using it. I don't really remember very much about the fight then. Actually, I don't think I saw much of it at all. That's how strong my master and Seniorious were—"

Slowly, he began to tell his tale.

In that dim, dark room.

So that they would be able to accept the girl's death.

So that they would be able to take the next step.

So that they would be able to survive their new life without Chtholly.

A Distant Dream, and Then...
-eternal dreamer-

By the time she realized it, the girl stood in a dark ruin.

Before her lay the dead body of a small child, a large open wound in her chest. The red blood that flowed out of it dyed the child's body a deep, murky red.

As she gazed down at it blankly, the child's outline suddenly blurred, and like tossing off old clothes, a half-transparent child herself stood there. The body still lay there, but the partially clear form of the child stood before her, looking at her.

Oh.

The child reached out.

Take it, I guess she means, the girl thought and gripped the child's hand with both of hers.

The child smiled.

The girl, too, smiled in turn.

They ran about, the child pulling the girl along.

The ruins were rather big, and it didn't seem like something that could be thoroughly explored with just a quick look around. Every time they turned a corner, every time they stepped over a broken door, there was something new lying there on the floor. There were stuffed animals in odd shapes, tattered and unreadable picture books, masses of crystal that she wasn't quite sure how to use but were probably recording crystals.

She spotted several things that looked interesting, but the child ignored them all and just pulled her farther and farther into the ruins.

She might be looking for something, the girl thought.

When she asked, the child nodded vigorously.

"Jay! Ebo!"

She didn't quite understand, but she seemed delighted and joyful, so what she mentioned must be some of her favorite things.

When she asked if they were somewhere in these ruins, the child cocked her head.

Maybe the question was too difficult for her. When that thought came to mind, she asked something else. Indeed, maybe it was what she should have asked in the first place.

What's your name?

"Elq!"

I see. Nice to meet you, Elq. That's a cute name.

She said with the slightest bit of flattery, and this time, the child pointed at the girl and tilted her head.

Are you asking for my name?

The child nodded, her head bobbing up and down.

What Elq said was right. She should give her own name after asking for the child's. This was a very reasonable line of thought.

My name.

My name is—

What's wrong? The girl was perplexed. She couldn't remember. It wasn't just her name. What was she? Why was she here? Where was *here* in the first place?

Elq tilted her head.

I— Right, that's right, I had something I needed to do. I had someone I needed to see. It's not the time for me to be wandering around here, at least.

So...so...

"...?"

Elq tilted her head again.

I have to go home, the girl announced. *There are people waiting for me, so I have to go where I need to be.*

"Do you have to?"

I have to.

"But there are so many bad things."

I know. But that doesn't matter.

There's someone I want to see. There's a reason I have to live on.

"Oh."

Elq looked down sadly, and after a short, contemplative silence, she let go of the girl's hand.

"Okay. See you, Chtholly."

—What?

✝

"—Huh?"

Chtholly woke up.

She slowly sat up. Fatigue from sleeping for too long enveloped her entire body.

She had a light headache, and she pressed against her temples.

She felt like she'd had a long dream. She couldn't remember it very well, but it was very...no, enormously nostalgic—and terrifying. That kind of dream.

No, there was something more important she needed to check first.

She patted herself. This body that she, with a few more curves, could call one of an adult. It was, without a doubt, Chtholly Nota Seniorious's own.

"I'm...alive—?"

Her mind was oddly clear, and there was even no trace of the torrent of those strange images. She panicked slightly—what did this mean?

There came a grotesque rumble.

She realized she was starving.

She should go to the kitchen and grab something.

When the idea crossed her mind and she exited to the hallway, she noticed that it was now nighttime, and it was raining outside. So the entire warehouse was wrapped in a quiet darkness—

She saw a faint light pouring from one room.

It was Nygglatho's room.

"…"

She unconsciously quieted her footsteps and neared the door.

"I wanted to make Chtholly happy."

Wha—?!

She heard something she couldn't glaze over, and her heart almost pounded out of her chest.

"Even if I couldn't, Seniorious is surrounded by tragedy and sadness. There was a time long ago when I wanted to do something about that. But I couldn't. My power was never enough, and it didn't change anything. I tried so hard and somehow managed to gain the strength to fight, but I had nothing more to show for that. I should have known. But in the end, I just couldn't let her go."

What? What? What?

What were they talking about here?

"And you're saying she likes something about this loser guy?"

There was Willem's voice, honestly puzzled.

What, you don't know such a simple thing? Chtholly felt a little mischievous.

You showed me so many firsts.

You first saved me in Tin Stalls Street. You first took me to a tower with such a beautiful view. You showed me so many expressions I'd never seen before. You drew out so many emotions I'd never felt before. You let me depend on you like no one else had, and you were the first to try and help me. You were the first to save me, the first to win against me, and—oh, I could never count them all.

So of course.

It's only natural that you're the first I fell in love with.

"—Notice that much, stupid."

Just as the quiet murmur escaped her lips—

"Aaaaaaaaahhhhhhhhhhhh!!"

There was a sudden, loud voice.

Her head snapped up, and there was Tiat, pointing straight at her with fear on her face.

"M-M-M-Miss Chtholly's gh-ghost?!"

Tiat's mouth opened and closed repeatedly, and her eyes were glazed over.

No! I'm alive! I'm not a ghost! So please be quiet! Willem will hear! She couldn't exactly yell that back, so instead she just waved her hands around but wasn't able to stop Tiat.

"Chthollyyyyyyyyy!"

She hugged her.

"You, you're a gh-ghost, but you're still Miss—Miss Chtholly!"

She clung her arms tightly around Chtholly's waist as a jumble of words tumbled from her mouth. It didn't look like she could get away. Well, it wasn't that she wanted to get away from the girl, but since she really didn't want the two in the room behind her to notice, she just wanted Tiat to be quiet—

As that was happening…

"—Chtholly…?"

She heard a hazy voice from behind her.

Slowly, guiltily, she turned around.

And of course, there he was.

"Uh, ummm…"

Willem was at a loss for words as he stood there completely still.

Was he sad? Was he happy? Was he angry? Was he none of the above? It was an expression she'd never seen before, a mix of all different emotions. Knowing that she was the cause of it, Chtholly, too, stood there silently.

"…I swear."

Of all the four who stood there in confusion, the first to make a move was Nygglatho. She lightly poked Willem's side with her elbow.

"Come now. You don't need to say anything heartfelt just yet. But don't you have something else to say first?"

"Uh… Oh, right."

Willem finally snapped out of it and took one step toward Chtholly.

"Welcome home, Chtholly."

That moment, Chtholly's entire body stopped working.

Her vision blurred, and she could no longer see; her chest tightened, and her breathing caught in her chest; her feet were rooted to the ground, and she couldn't walk; her mind went white, and she couldn't think; her throat wavered, and she couldn't speak.

"Ah…uh…"

—I'm back. I'm home.

It was simply those words that would not become sound.

She wanted so badly to say them. She had been ready to say them.

She'd made up her mind to appeal to him with kindness the best she could if she saw him again. But when she stood in front of the man himself, she could do nothing.

Her feet tangled themselves…or so she thought.

Her jumbled senses aside, it was only her balance that seemed to be working. A moment's sensation of floating. The second she thought she would fall over, her whole body was enveloped in a feeling of warmth.

"Really, welcome home."

From the warmth that wrapped around her came, of all things, words that warmed her soul.

They completely broke her.

She couldn't see, couldn't hear. She couldn't breathe, couldn't walk, couldn't think, couldn't talk.

She simply surrendered to the impulse that welled up from deep within her heart—

—and, with a loud voice, began to cry.

One after the other, the little faeries came from their rooms, sleepily rubbing their eyes in curiosity, and gathered in the hallway.

The many young gazes showered Chtholly as she cried like a baby.

"...The miracle of love?" Nephren tilted her head.

"Love or not, it's obviously a miracle. We'll probably need to pay back big time for this one. Knowing that girl, she's probably paid for it already without a thought for the future...," Ithea murmured, tears pooling behind her smile.

Chtholly's voice, tired from crying, quieted at last and became a hushed sob.

Her stomach growled loudly.

Afterword/
An Actual Afterword

Sorry to keep you waiting. I am a not-so-new author, Kareno.

Here is the second volume of *What* (the rest omitted), a laid-back, relaxing slice-of-life tale about a retired old hero living among a large group of girls in the countryside. I'm not lying.

To give the worst spoilers for those who like to read the afterword first, Chtholly never says, "I'm home." I'm not lying.

Now, book three will take place in the faerie warehouse again. I am thinking of making it a triple feature of *Chtholly's Medical Treatment Diary*, *Happy Beastie Paradise*, and *Farewell Brave ~Another Loss at Dawn~*... But in reality, the sales of Volume 1 just after it was released were apparently not very good, so as of now I cannot promise a third volume. To put it bluntly, all merchandise, not just novels, may not exist if they don't sell. So on the contrary, with the support and help of those who want to read the rest of the girls' story, then our path will be opened. No, I'm serious.

I pray that we meet again on the opened path, at the faerie warehouse of tomorrow.

Fall 2014
AKIRA KARENO

Discover the other side of Magic High School—read the light novel!

The Irregular at MagicHigh School

Explore the world from Tatsuya's perspective as he and Miyuki navigate the perils of First High and more! Read about adventures only hinted at in *The Honor Student at Magic High School*, and learn more about all your favorite characters. This is the original story that spawned a franchise!